C000104401

THE MISTRESS AND THE SLAVE

THE MISTRESS
AND
THE SLAVE

A MASOCHIST REALISTIC LOVE STORY

ATHENS   MCMV

IMPRINTED FOR ITS MEMBERS BY

THE EROTIKA BIBLION SOCIETY

First published 1905

This Facsimile Edition published by Delectus Books,
London, England

Copyright © Delectus Books 1995
Introduction © Michael R. Goss 1995

Delectus Books
27 Old Gloucester Street
London WC1N 3XX

ISBN 1 897767 09 9

Printed by Woolnough Ltd.,
Irthlingborough, Northhamptonshire

INTRODUCTION

This superb Edwardian novel was first published in English back in 1905 by "The Erotica Biblion Society", a teaming up of Leonard Charles Smithers and his friend and business partner Harry Sidney Nichols.

Smithers was a solicitor and Nichols a bookseller and printer. Both moved from their native Sheffield to London apparently because of the easy availability of dangerously young girls.[1]

The Mistress & the Slave was translated from a French novel *La Maitresse et L'Esclave* first published by Maison Mystere, Bruxelles (probably Paris) around 1903, a publishing company ran by Charles Hirsch (c.1889-c.1939). Hirsch was also a renowned bookseller who certainly knew Smithers & Nichols and supplied the collector, and former Private Case custodian, C.R. Dawes with much of his collection of fine erotica. Dawes later commented in 1943:

"There was, up to the outbreak of war in 1939, - and hope still is - a charming old gentleman in Paris, M. Charles Hirsch,[2] who is a great authority on erotica, having dealt in it more or less all his life, and always treated his business seriously and intelligently. In 1889 he came to London opened a shop for the sale of continental books and newspapers in Coventry Street, where he remained for some years. On his return to Paris, he had a delightful shop in the Rue des Pyramides, and afterwards in the Palais Royal. In his Coventry Street days, M. Hirsch knew (Oscar) Wilde who was a customer of his...."

The translation was possibly by Smithers or by Nichols who, was then based in Paris running books for Charles Carrington, or even a third candidate, Reginald Bacchus, theatrical journalist and author of another

Smithers/Nichols production *The Confessions of Nemesis Hunt*. There is no information as to who wrote the original French edition although it may be reasonable to speculate that Charles Hirsch himself may have had a hand in the books creation. Evidence shows that the original edition was probably printed in London by Wooley and Lamplugh, at Lamplugh's establishment in Dalling Road, Hammersmith, where other erotic novels, along with piracies of Oscar Wilde, were also produced.

The publishers original prospectus for the English edition is worth reproducing here in full:

READY IN SEPTEMBER 1905. The Mistress and the Slave is a realistic masochist novel, written with great power. It is a story of modern times, its scene is laid in Paris, and it relates the ascendancy which a woman of the lower class gets over a man of position and wealth. The perversity of her nature, with its absolute domination over him, eventually culminates in a tragic ending. The book consists of about 160pp. crown 8Vo, is printed on good paper, and the edition is limited to 200 copies. The Subscription price is £2.2.0 per copy.

A number of prospectuses for the various French editions were reproduced in Louis Perceau's *Bibliographie du Roman Erotique* (1930) and are worth consulting for bibliophiles.

The text of *The Mistress and The Slave*, while not having the finesse of books such as *A Guide to The Correction of Young Gentlemen*, *The Romance of Chastisement* or *Gynecocracy* is surprisingly direct and advanced in the intricacies and balance of power of the mistress/slave relationship as this excerpt clearly shows:

But, my child, you don't seem to understand what a mistress is. For instance: your child your favourite daughter, might be dying and I should send you to the Bastille to get me a twopenny trinket. You would go, you would obey! Do you understand?" - "Yes!" he murmured, so pale and troubled that he could scarcely breathe. "And you will do everything I wish?" - "Everything, darling mistress! Everything! I swear it to you!"

It's more forthright, explicit and occasionally brutal nature along with such quaint Victorian expressions as spend, cockstand and frigg, though somewhat anachronistic in our current age add a certain charm to this delightfully written and occasionally romantic novel.

The Mistress and the Slave remains long neglected, at last revived by the Delectus Classics of Erotic Literature series.

1. *A brief account of the careers of Smithers and Nichols is given in the introduction to another Delectus publication "The Petticoat Dominant", for which they were also responsible.*

2. *Further information on Hirsch can be found in Peter Mendes superb book "Clandestine Erotic Fiction in English 1800-1930: A Bibliographical Study. Scolar Press Aldershot 1993.*

MICHAEL R. GOSS
London 1995

I

HER fat arms naked, the servant was perched up on a chair. She was cleaning the window with a chamois leather. And each time that she raised herself up to reach higher, her thick serge petticoat drew up, uncovering her nervous and muscular legs.

She was a tall, strapping lass, a brunette with a hard expression, and thirty years old at most.

Undoubtedly erotic ideas were exciting her. For she stopped working and looked out into the street. Then she passed her pointed tongue over her red, fleshy lips, bent her loins, stretched out her arms, and finished by lightly rubbing her nipples with her open hands in a furtive caress.

The door opened, and a little boy of eight or nine years of age came into the room. A light-haired little chap, quite out of breath from having run up two flights of stairs.

"What do you want, George?" asked the servant nonchalantly.

9

"Oh, Mélanie, are you there? I say, you haven't
seen my punchinello, have you? Where is it?"

"Wait a bit, I'll find it for you."

She got down from the chair and came deliberately
to George with a heavy footstep; the parquet squeaked
beneath her foot. She took the child by his shoulder
and bent him back. Unbuttoning his trousers she let
them drop down. And raising his shirt she took hold
of his prick between her thumb and first finger, whilst
with her other fingers she tickled his tiny balls.

"Here is your punchinello," exclaimed the big girl
laughingly.

Little by little the member grew erect.

The astonished child, very pale, stuck his stomach
out, groaning:

"Mélanie, what are you doing? Stop, stop, I feel
quite funny. Oh, I beg you, let me go."

"Be quiet, silly, you are going to see how good it
is."

George was silent; a feeble moaning, almost a groan,
that was all.

He had fallen on his knees, his neck stiffened. And
he stuck out his stomach desperately, looking persistently at the movements of the big, naked arm.

The big girl bent over the child, frigged him quickly,
rubbing his gland with her fingers.

George groaned gently, and all his body twisted

itself up, his head fell backwards in a convulsion, and he closed his eyes, thinking that he was going to die.

Without discharging, he felt the spasm.

He got up. Full of fear and anguish he stood trembling in front of Mélanie, who, with arms akimbo, laughed with a coarse laugh which shook her whole body.

"That was good, wasn't it?" she finished by saying. "But that is nothing yet, I shall shew you lots of other things."

Quite giddy, he did not reply, but fastened up his clothes awkwardly.

She sat on the edge of the bed, and, pulling up her petticoat and chemise, shewed him her belly.

She called George to her.

Still very moved, the child approached her.

She let herself drop backwards, and, with her finger, she indicated her clitoris.

"You are going to suck that like a barley-sugar stick. You will suck until I tell you 'Enough'; go on."

George felt himself squeezed between Mélanie's legs, and bent docilely over her vulva. But the thick, dark hair frightened him, and the strong smell made him sick.

He drew back.

"No, I don't want to."

"Yes, yes, little one," supplicated the servant, "come on."

He struggled, exhausting himself in sterile efforts, imprisoned by her powerful legs. All the same he was obstinate, and pushed his hands against Mélanie's knees to get loose.

"No, leave me alone."

"I tell you, you shall do it," scolded Mélanie.

"If you don't let me go," replied George resolutely, "I shall speak to Mama. After all, you are not mistress here; you are only the servant."

With a thrust Mélanie sent the child rolling into the middle of the room, and sprang up herself to her full height. Her thick eyebrows contracted, her nostrils quivered, she dominated him.

"What do you say? Just say it again. Ah, I am only a servant! Take that! and that! and that!"

Each exclamation was punctuated with a good smack. The frightened child did not utter a cry.

"Wait, I'll shew you!"

She seized him by the nape of the neck, and, in spite of his struggles, she bent his head between her knees, took down his trousers in a twinkling, and gave him a sound thrashing on his bare bottom. The blows echoed thick and hard.

George howled.

"Hold your tongue," she commanded.

And she brutally thrust a finger into his anus.

"Oh, oh," he cried in a voice choked by pain. "Forgive me, Mélanie, my dear Mélanie. What are you doing? You are tearing me! I will do everything you wish. Oh, please forgive me!"

"I'll forgive you by-and-bye, but try to cry out again!" And once more her heavy hand beat on his little bottom.

In spite of the pain the child contrived to stifle his cries, and groaned lamentably. Through his tears he stared fixedly at her calves, swelling out her white stockings.

Reversing her hand, Mélanie turned him over, and frigged him again, whilst he supplicated:

"Mélanie, my good Mélanie, stop, I beg of you! Oh, Mélanie, everything, everything that you want, everything, everything, I swear it; but stop, do stop!"

He was already spending, his eyes rolling and his stomach jutted out.

"Oh, Mélanie, what must I do, tell me?"

She lay down again tranquilly on the edge of the bed, put a pillow under her head, pulled up her frock, and shewed him her clitoris.

"Suck."

He bent over it, panting.

With his heart full, and his eyes streaming with tears, he sucked greedily.

13

"Harder," commanded Mélanie briefly, "harder."

The child sucked with all his might; suddenly he stopped, quivering with sickness. His mouth was filled with a bitter taste. The servant had spent. He wished to pull his head away, but the girl was watching. She seized him by the hair and held him firmly. As he tried to draw back she gave him a blow, and then pulled his ear roughly. The terrified child recommenced sucking.

"Enough," cried Mélanie, and, pushing him away, she re-adjusted herself. Then she took him on her knees, and petted him tenderly.

"Well, what do you say about it?" she asked curiously.

George's only reply was to throw his arms round her neck, and cover her face with mad kisses.

She bent his head back, looked at him with a good-natured smile, and, placing a rough kiss on his lips, she gently caressed the child's prick.

Suddenly she pushed him away again.

"That's enough for to-day," she declared, "to-morrow you will refuse to get up. You will say that you have got a headache, and you will not go to school. In the afternoon, when I am doing the rooms, you will come and join me here."

But the excited child pressed himself against her, full of desire, wishing for further caresses. He rubbed himself against her petticoats, and did not want to go away.

Mélanie had to speak to him in her hard, rough voice to make him leave her. Then she spoke to him tenderly, with her voice full of promises.

"Come, little one, be a good boy. If you come to-morrow, you shall see how good it will be."

George went away regretfully and slowly; he turned round at the door, and looked long at her with imploring eyes.

She smiled nicely at him, and with a bound he was back to her.

Then she got cross. "You'll finish by annoying me. I have told you to be off. Are you going to obey me? If not, look out for your bottom; it will be a different thing from just now."

Before her threatening hand he recoiled, upset.

On the stairs he became aware how upset he was; he stopped to take breath, and assumed a composed air. When he went into the dining-room no one noticed anything.

Next day after breakfast when he saw Mélanie, who was doing the rooms, his heart beat, but he managed to appear calm. That morning she had said to him in that rough voice which made him tremble :

"You will come and join me this afternoon. But

you must wait a bit. Above all, don't be stupid enough
to follow me at once."

He began to play. He took out his lead soldiers
and arranged them in battle order. Intent on his
game, he forgot Mélanie.

All at once she stood in front of him. She had come
downstairs under the pretext—"Madam, I have no
more brass polish."

Whilst his mother was feeling in her purse, George
lowered his eyes, and bent his head before the servant's
imperious look.

He hastened to replace the soldiers in their box ; his
hands trembled so much that he could not put the lid
on the box, and, as soon as he knew Mélanie had gone
back, he ran upstairs to join her.

"Is it thus that you obey me? You deserve your
little prick pulling off."

He caressed her, stroking her face with his little
hands, and implored her in a sweet and quivering
voice, choked with emotion.

"All right, let it pass this time, but don't let it
happen again."

She took him in her robust arms, raised him, and laid
him along the bed.

"Don't move; I'm going to do something good to
you."

She unbuttoned him. She had no need to work

it; it was already standing. She sucked it tranquilly.

The child writhed like a worm under the too keen
pleasure. With his little hands he desperately tried to
push away her head, her murderous mouth, but he had
to submit to the caress until its end.

When Mélanie raised her head he did not move.
He lay all in a heap, his head buried in the pillows,
looking at her with rounded eyes, with big, frightened
eyes.

"Fie, the molly coddle!" she cried. "He is killed
because I have done Mimi to him. Get up. You are
going to lick my arse."

She lifted him from the bed and stood him up. Then
she bent over in front of the bed, placing her hands on
it, with her petticoats raised.

"Go behind me," she ordered, "and take care to
stick your tongue right in my arsehole. As far as ever
you can. You will lick my shit as you lick the jam off
your bread and butter."

The child quivered in every limb, and resisted. He
remained terrified before her enormous rounded buttocks.
And all the slit was yellow; there was even some of it
on the buttocks. Again he thought of resisting. But
without changing her position, she had but to turn her
head, and fix him with her big, wicked eyes to make
him give in.

He set himself to work. He licked with all his strength, pushing his tongue in as far as he could.

The girl sighed with pleasure. A strange smell, a heady taste, intoxicated George. He still licked. Then he commenced to suck, and placing his slender hand on her vulva, he tickled her clitoris. Mélanie laughed with a nervous laugh. In spite of his fatigue, George went on licking. His mouth filled with saliva, which ran out and trickled slowly down the valley between the big buttocks as far as the vagina, and then ran over his hand, but he did not stop sucking or tickling.

"Stop, stop," the servant sighed.

She cried out with pleasure. But in his turn he was obstinate, and would not leave her before she had spent.

However, she finished by escaping from him.

She kissed him full on the mouth, and frigged him very gently with rapid vibrations of the wrist, scarcely perceptible, his entire prick buried in her large hand.

She then sent him away.

Next day, Saturday, George again remained in the house, which enabled him after breakfast to run upstairs to Mélanie. On Sunday also she sucked him, and made him suck her. Then she lay on the bed, drew George between her legs, and provoked the spasm by rubbing the child's prick against her clitoris.

On Monday he had to make up his mind to go to school.

But, during the evening, in the kitchen at the sink, where he had gone to wash his hands, George found himself alone with Mélanie. Without unbuttoning him, she seized hold of his prick through the cloth of his trousers, and frigged him vigorously.

"Will you hurry up?" she said to him. "Spend! Hurry up!"

This was a rapid and delicious enjoyment, which left him enervated and stupified for the entire evening.

And during two months George was tossed off every day. He was always seeking an opportunity of being alone with Mélanie in some corner or other.

On Thursday and Sunday afternoons he slipped up the staircase to be with her whilst she did the rooms. Then his great happiness was to creep inside her petti-coats, and remain there silent,—so happy that he could have passed hours there if she would have allowed him to do so.

She was on a chair cleaning the windows. He slipped underneath her frock. He remained standing, and saw her fat calves in front of him. He stood there, motionless, almost in ecstasy, sniffing fervently the stink of her vulva and her buttocks. He also tried to put his hand on them, but whilst she was working the servant did not like larking, and she forbade him to move, in a tone so severe that he never dared recommence.

However, when she was in a good temper, sometimes she condescended to laugh a little.

"Attention, George! Climb on the chair so that I can fart in your nose."

George hastened to obey.

He climbed on the chair. Stooping a little, his face was at the height of her buttocks. Mélanie let a sonorous fart. The chair quivered under the shock. George, half suffocated, his mouth and nose full of the fetid aroma, had to cling to the servant's knees so as not to fall.

Only when she had finished her work, did she occupy herself with the child. She sucked him, and made him suck her; or she frigged his prick with her clitoris.

However, George's mother got alarmed.

The child's fresh-coloured complexion had disappeared. He had now a leaden look, his eyes hollow with black marks round them. Sometimes, he ate greedily and voraciously, but loathing his food as he swallowed it.

In the full autumn sun he quivered with cold and fever. The doctor at first thought he was growing too quickly. However, he ended by asking George questions when he was alone with him. He wanted to know if the child had any "bad habits."

The little one did not understand him. When the doctor explained, he blushed. Thinking about Mélanie, he hesitated. The doctor was expecting a confession, when, with an accent which sounded like truth, George declared that he had no "bad habits."

The doctor praised him, told him to keep from them, and exposed to him all the fatal consequences of masturbation.

He advised change of air, physical exercise, and a journey where George would find a healthy fatigue through taking long walks.

So the family prepared for their annual holiday. They decided to go to the Rhine. George's father was prevented by business from going : his eldest sister stopped to look after the house. His mother, his two other sisters and his eldest brother went with him.

The novelty, the scenery flitting by the side of the train, filled George with delight. But from the first night at the hotel he became gloomy, thinking always of Mélanie's hand. Little by little the idea obsessed him. It appealed more and more. The child felt his hand go there by itself, ready to wander. Then he remembered what the doctor had said to him. The charm was broken. In spite of the torment of his young flesh, he resisted. Sleep came, peaceable, refreshing.

When the family had been away about a week, a letter came to them from Mayence, with news of their house. His big brother read it aloud. And George grew attentive when he heard what his eldest sister had written. When rebuked for not doing her work properly, Mélanie had replied insolently, and had been turned out. George's heart was full. They went to table. In spite of a dish of peaches and large bunches of grapes, he looked awry during the whole of dinner.

If at night, alone in bed, he again thought of Mélanie, he was yet able to resist the temptation. He did not masturbate himself.

Years rolled on. Intelligent and quickly grasping things, George was but a mediocre scholar. Disorderly and vagabond, he loved playing truant, but he read much, and stored up much knowledge.

Open air life, his contempt of bad weather, his application to sports, made him grow up a tall and robust youth.

When he was eighteen years old, a woman of thirty-five, a friend of the family, wished to initiate him. She was arch and pretty, with a blonde's frail delicacy. With her he knew love simple and sentimental, insipid caresses, a long rigmarole of kisses and of coition, intermingled with poetic raptures.

He had other mistresses. They seemed haughty and proud. But immediately they had given themselves to him, they weakened, and became submissive. Those who loved him tired him with their docility. He became dictatorial with women, even bullying them.

They loved him all the more for it. However, when making love to them he was insinuating and supple, attentive, lavishing little attentions to excess on them. He was witty, and knew how to make them laugh. They adored him. But those whom he had the most ardently desired, even the most seductive, seemed to him banal after the first night. Speedily, in spite of their attractions, satiety paralysed his flesh.

He was struck with a tall strong woman. Afterwards he was disabused. She had enormous limbs, but it was all fat. Nay more, she cooed like a dove, and pretended to be ashamed, even in bed.

Then it was the turn of a female athlete, a strapping wench, who would take a man on at wrestling. But, when they were intimate together, she shewed herself so humble that he got disgusted. Under some absurd pretext, he boxed her ears. She hid her head behind her arm, like the little girls do.

He had dancers who, to distract his thoughts, lifted their leg in the air whilst he spoke of love to them. He knew singers who dinned a refrain in his ears, whilst asking for bread at the supper-table. He took work-girls out walking in the outskirts on Sundays.

He associated himself with sensualists and idealists. And when these women had done "mimi"[1] to him,

[1] "Mimi"—a slang term to designate sucking the sexual parts of a man or woman with the lips.—*Trans.*

they thought they had granted him the supreme refinement of love. The women of the brothels asked him
what his passion was. At times he slept with a cocotte.
In her luxury of chiffons she seemed duller to him than
an ordinary woman. He had, like a homesickness, a
regret of sensations of which he had an unformed idea.
But he could not express his wishes to himself. They
were so vague !

If he thought of Mélanie, which rarely happened to
him, it was with disdain. And indeed, he would willingly have returned her the floggings she had given
him.

He had left his sad northern town, got established,
and was prospering in business. And he swore to
himself to remain a bachelor, to live a joyous single
life, his library full of rare and curious books, his cellar
filled with fine wines.

Then he met a young girl with whom he fell seriously
in love. She was pretty, with an imperious and delicate
beauty, witty and easy in her manner.

At first the senses alone were aroused in George.
He wanted her for his mistress. And as she was poor,
pity and tenderness added themselves to his love.

He married her. Immediately, his passion became
extravagant. But he dared not show the depth of it.
It was an excess of tolerated sensuality, of permitted
appetite. However, the virgin grew frightened. She

was always docile, despite the slumber of her flesh.   At
the end of several months George became less exuberant,
and the young wife, clasped in his arms, uttered a cry.
She had had the revelation of the supreme joy.

She then became the passionate one of the two.
George always loved her, but he avoided coition.   She
was not disheartened, she saw in him the lover and the
husband, the master whom she ought blindly to obey.
Children were born to them : two girls at an interval of
a year.   Little by little George's passions cooled ; his
senses calmed, he performed the conjugal duty with
indifference, and laughed at his wife's transports, and
checked her fiery impulses.

Thus he arrived at the age of forty.   Fencing, boxing,
swimming, and riding had kept him in excellent con-
dition, and muscular.   He looked young, and was
good looking.   But women no longer interested him !

II

At forty years of age George was well enough off to give a large dowry to his two daughters, the elder of whom was then eighteen.

He could now think about himself. Arrived at the age of ambition, and of a practical mind, he canvassed for middle-class but lucrative honours.

At Belleville, where he had a good chance of being elected, he put up as a candidate for the municipal council. This very evening, at a meeting, he had explained to his electors, turbulent and credulous workmen, an entire programme of social revolution, and had squandered litres of beer on them.

His audience had applauded him, carried him in triumph. It was near midnight before he was able to break away from the faithful members of his committee. He left them with the beer-jugs at their lips in the large brasserie of the quartier.

When he found himself alone at the corner of the Boulevard de la Villette and the Faubourg du Temple, he breathed easily. He felt the walk would do him good, and decided not to go home by rail. He was cheerfully going down the Faubourg, when at the corner of the Rue St. Maur he jostled against a group which was going up towards Belleville. Two men—obviously young ponces—and two women without hats. One of them was insignificant, insipid, and faded; the other, a tall and beautiful girl, plump and delicate, was clad poorly with a desperate coquetry.

As she passed by George, she saw him looking at her. She fixed her large brown eyes upon him, giving them such an intense expression of voluptuousness that George trembled. He stood where he was, as though glued to the ground. The pretty girl smiled in a ravishing manner, and turning, she went towards him. But shaking his head, he went on his way without looking back.

However, she went in pursuit of him. At the corner of the Avenue Parmentier she stepped in front of him.

"Won't you come?"

"No."

She insisted, barring his way with her tall figure, extended and flexible. And, again approaching him, she grazed against him, stomach against stomach, caressing him with her breath. He moved away: she followed. She seemed to unite herself to him, and the warmth of her young flesh, penetrating through his

27

clothing, gave him a strange languorous feeling. She exhaled a heady scent, which recalled vaguely the perfume of sandal-wood, and which utterly unnerved him. However, he tried to get away. But whether he recoiled to the right or to the left, she moved forward on either haunch, and he saw nothing but her face before him, quite close to his. A pretty face. Very pretty. The arab type in a Parisian setting. A white skin, strewn with freckles. In addition she had a strange look, promising superhuman delights, which gave him a curious feeling. And he felt these eyes, these eyes so beautiful, sink profoundly into him. He felt his senses leaving him, he struggled in a whirlpool. His entire being was swallowed up: his brain swam.

"Come along! you will see how nice it can be!"

The thought ran through his mind—If his electors saw him!

"No!" he said, in a firm voice.

He moved away from her, drawing backwards. He was already going, when she swiftly moved her hand forward, gave him a rapid adroit caress, and assured herself that he had an erection. And she did not remove her hand, but pressed more tightly.

He started, and implored her, in a tearful voice.

"No! I don't want—Leave me. I beg of you!"

She glanced at him, curiously. A cruel smile curled her lip, uncovering her sharp white teeth—the teeth of a young wolf. Then her expressive face again changed. She had a hard authoritative manner. She commanded briefly.

"Come!"

And she walked forward, without looking back, certain of being obeyed. And he fell into step with her. He walked along, reeling. His entire body was shaking.

She stopped, and rang at the door of a cheap hotel. And when the door opened she went in, saying to George:

"Come in!"

He still hesitated. She passed a hand behind him, again knowing exactly where to tickle him. He went forward. And, all the length of the staircase, she incited him with her expert hand.

A waiter joined them, and opened a door.

"No!" exclaimed the girl. "A room with a fire in it."

"There isn't one!" the waiter replied.

She shrugged her shoulders, pushed George into the room, and seized the candlestick from the waiter's hands.

"Give him twenty sous!" she said.

The waiter went away. She turned the key in the lock.

"I was wrong to bring you to this filthy hole. You have a swell look about you. You must love comfort, and a fireless room can't inspire you greatly. But you know, my doggy, I had no choice. Smart rooms are wanting in the quartier. Another time we will go elsewhere. We shall see each other again, shan't we? And now, give me my little present, it will be very good of you."

Before this chatter George was silent. He was feeling uncomfortable and bored. However, he remained, perplexed. What ought he to give her? He looked round him. Everything was miserable and questionable. He had a hundred sous loose in his pocket, and he handed them to the girl.

"What's this?" she said. "I thought you were a smart man. Make it up to a louis."

Decidedly the charm was broken. There was nothing left to do but to hurry away—to get off! He threw a twenty francs piece on the table, and went towards the door. Immediately the girl was there before him.

With a turn of her hand she had unbuttoned him. She held his prick. With a finger nail on the bridle, her fingers were put in motion. A caress, at once energetic and sweet The nail remained immoveable, and her fingers scarcely moved, with a jerk, a rapid vibration of the wrist.

George was surprised and unquiet before her profound look, charged with a sombre flame. The back of her neck attracted him. He breathed this undefinable perfume which came from her skin, and which finished by intoxicating him.

He sought her lips, hoping to kiss her full on the mouth. And encircling her round and thin waist, he tried to draw her to the bed. She avoided the kiss, and resisted his attempt. She frigged him with the same light, even movement.

He stammered: "What is your name?"

"Anna."

"What a pleasant name! It pronounces your beauty, and sounds like the trump of victory."

She smiled—"Flatterer—and yours?"

"George."

"That is a nice name also."

She pressed her nail a little harder, and accelerated the movement of her wrist.

"Come!" he sighed. "Oh! come!"

"No! You are going to spend like this!"

He felt a shock, experienced a real fright.

"Ah! not that way!"

He took her by the arm, wishing to push her away, to disengage himself. But his will-power was annihilated, his muscles remained flaccid. His fingers slipped along this arm, whose firm curves they pressed, under her stuff gown.

She increased the quickness of her wrist's movements, and her nail sank into the flesh. Slowly she brought on the pleasure, irritating his desire to frenzy. This woman's nail seemed to George harder than steel; it burnt him, sinking in right to his marrow.

He began to implore:

" I beg of thee, come and make love."

" No! I want to tame thee. Thou shalt be my slave. To start with, I forbid thee to tutoyer [1] me."

He reeled, and began to groan: " Yes! But at least a kiss. A single one! A kiss! A kiss!"

She shook her head as a sign of refusal, and continued the same gentle and rapid movement. Her hand kept in the same position, with its slow and inexorable advance towards the spasm.

He was breathless. His eyes stuck out, and he trembled in every limb. Already he felt wet. The juice of the prostate gland was oozing away under the too intense excitement.

" I cannot! I cannot!" he groaned.

With a prompt and vigorous gesture, she placed her foot on the table, drew up her petticoat, and uncovered a strong and well-shaped leg.

" Look what a pretty leg I have got."

He looked passionately at her leg, with distraught eyes. She tightened her grasp, increased her jerking

[1] The use of the second person singular, *thou* and *thee*, is usual in France between lovers and intimate friends.

movement, and her nail wounded the bridle of his penis.

He bawled out: "Anna! Anna! Thou art killing me. . . . Darling Anna!"

The sperm sprang out in jets under the girl's fingers. George felt his knees giving way under him. At last she left him, and going to the wash stand she washed her hands. Then putting the basin on the floor, she bent over it, and made her toilette, pulling her clothes up high. George peeped at her, curious to see what her body was like. He had never seen a croup like hers, with its tight division, and its rebounding buttocks.

She began chattering to him.

"You will come to-morrow. You see I make love well. You 've spent well, haven't you?"

"It is curious," he replied. "I would not have believed that a woman could have gone to the end, and make me spend like a child."

"It is because you have me already in your blood, little one. I saw that well enough when you tried to push me away. You had taken hold of my arm. It was not worth your while struggling against me. All that I wish to do to thee, I shall do. You cannot prevent me. To-morrow we will go somewhere else. Do you know any place which is better than this? Give me a rendezvous!"

"At the Madeleine? Wilt thou?"

She resumed her severe air.

" I have forbidden thee to call me 'thou,' once for all. Why ? That is not thy business. I have my reason."

He felt disconcerted, not knowing whether to be annoyed or to laugh. However, he obeyed her.

" At the Madeleine, at nine o'clock, at the omnibus office. Will that suit you ? "

"Quite. I will be there. And now, come here, and I will wash you."

The girl poured the water jug on his member from a height, holding it gracefully. Then she looked contemptuously at the towel.

" Not with this dish-cloth. Give me your handkerchief."

She did not finish wiping him. The movement of her fingers excited him; and as he bent over her, he smelt her perfume strongly. He had an erection. A desire again made his senses wander.

" I beg of thee—I beg of thee, come. Why refuse me ? "

She shook her head, and sat at the side of the bed. Her pulled-up petticoats uncovered her legs. She enveloped him with her lascivious look.

" To-morrow."

" Would you like a hundred francs ? "

" Give them."

He handed her the money. She folded the bank-note and thrust it in her bodice. He went towards her, his hands stretched out, ready to take her. She stood upright, with a contemptuous air.

"I have told thee: to-morrow. Don't insist."

He knelt down and implored her, rubbing his face against her knees. And he began to lick her slippers, repeating her name in a dolorous and long drawn out litany. She did not move, but appeared indifferent. However, she ended by getting impatient.

"Are you going to finish this farce?"

He got up and tried to put his arms round her again, and succeeded in getting his ears soundly boxed. In his boxing matches he had certainly had more violent blows, and thumps quite as severe from the hard and vigorous fists of men, and had not been upset by them. But this sweet womanly hand terrified him. He implored, "Anna! Pardon! Pardon!"

She opened the door, "Be off!"

"But you will come to-morrow?"

"Yes, yes!"

He went away. She remained, standing upright in the doorway. As he was going downstairs, she called him: "George!"

He turned round, delighted. She glanced at him with her strange look, her look of a lustful woman, desiring the embrace of the male. He uttered a cry of joy. But, as he thought he had her in his arms, she burst out laughing, and slammed the door in his face. He knocked : "Open! Open!"

"Shit!" she cried in her fresh and sonorous voice.

He went off rapidly. He had never been so upset. Oh! how he desired her, this strange woman!

The cold air did him good, and the walk also helped to calm him. He was able to reflect. From every side the adventure seemed to him without issue. It was better to end this freak. To begin again would be foolish. He would certainly not go to the rendezvous. Yet already he regretted missing its expected delights. He pleaded for and against. The struggle he had with himself seemed the best argument. If he did not act it would be too late. As she had warned him, he would become her slave. That word made him laugh. He lifted his head proudly, and puffed out his chest, swollen with great aspirations. He felt himself strong, a dictator,—what likelihood was there that a little girl would abase him? However, it was best not to play with danger. Decidedly he would never see her again, little street-walker. Let her cool her toes, waiting.

He had reached the boulevard St. Denis, when the shadow of a woman made him tremble. In spite of their unlikeness, he thought he recognised Anna. He started running. It was not she. A prostitute dressed entirely in satin, who, having finished her night's work, was calling a cab. She looked at George. Smiling amiably at him, she beckoned to him. He deliberately got into the cab and sat at her side. The cabman went rapidly to her house. "What is thy name?" asked George.

"Emilie."—"Ah!" said he, already disappointed.

She pressed herself against him, coaxingly. Although he scarcely wanted to, he put his arm round her. Then she abandoned herself to him, and held out her lips. He had to close his eyes. No! it was not Anna! The cab stopped. He paid the cabman, gave a ten francs piece to the woman, and went off, leaving her so nonplussed that she could not find a word. He was quite close to the St. Lazare station. He took the underground railway to the Porte Maillot. And in two minutes he was at home, in the Rue Le Sueur. His wife was still waiting up.

He had to relate his evening's work. She smiled, delighted. Her George had been applauded, carried in triumph. How well he merited it! Was he not the most beautiful, the most intelligent, the strongest of men? George felt his heart swell at being loved like this. He felt the pride of the male, virile and protecting love. Whilst chatting, he undressed. He slipped at her side. She coaxed him, pinched his neck and his muscles with a caress which formerly, at the time of his great passion for her, had infatuated him. He remembered their happy days, and chastely they had connection with each other. He looked long and tenderly at his wife. How pretty she was! What a delicate style of beauty! with the prettiness of a miniature! equally desirous as this Venus of the cross-roads!

From that moment it was finished. He felt that if he again thought of this woman, he would never be able to go to the end of the caress. And he hastened his movements, giving formidable blows of his loins. However the obsession persisted. He closed his eyes, and succeeded in spending, by imagining that Anna was there, and that she commanded him to do so. His wife also was possessed by the same spasm, and groaned with pleasure. As for him, he remained silent. He had enjoyed stupidly, without any pleasure, and felt rancorous, as though he had been defiled. She let her head fall on his breast, stroking his face with her hands

" How good it was, darling ! "

He thrust her away, full of cold rage.

" You stifle me. I am going to get up."

" Where are you going ? " she said, astonished.

"I am going to sleep in the spare room. And in future it will be my room."

She burst out crying. Tears ran down her cheeks, without a sob. This mute grief exasperated him.

" But, understand—it is foolish. I am exhausted— you know a political meeting is very tiring. One has to make speeches, to discuss things. When you think everything is finished, it all begins over again. It's overwhelming. I come home disposed to sleep well, to refresh myself for to-morrow, and I play the goat! Devil take it! everything at its time. Let us leave this alone until after the elections."

He had pulled on his trousers, and put his slippers on. She cried out, her voice broken by sobs, "George! my beloved George——"

But he had gone, discontented with everything, and furious against himself. He went to bed, and thoroughly decided: he would not commit the folly of seeing this girl again. When he came down to breakfast the bad night which he had passed had made his temper worse. His wife was, as always, thoughtful and sweet. But her face looked worn, and her eyes were reddened. He felt sorry and was vexed with himself for his sensitiveness. He bullied everybody. However, business matters came to distract his thoughts; but towards evening he became feverishly agitated. Every minute he pulled his watch out, and then blushed at the reason he had for doing so. He telegraphed that he should not be home for dinner, and went to one of the large restaurants on the boulevards. But it was with difficulty he forced himself to swallow a few mouthfuls, his throat was so contracted. He saw his face swollen in the mirror, and his heart thumped loudly. Then it occurred to him that he had not sufficient money on him

He had, purposely, left his purse at the office. But he had his cheque book on him. He counted his money. It came to one hundred and twenty-seven francs. His bill paid, he had not five louis left. He filled in a cheque and gave it to the waiter. As he was known there, he had no difficulty in getting it cashed. But he would not have a note for five hundred francs, and insisted on gold. It was only eight o'clock. In his impatience, he had hurried through his dinner. Smoking his cigar, he strolled along the boulevard, stopping before the shop-fronts. As he was looking in a jeweller's window an idea came to him. He was just going inside when it occurred to him that he would find a better shop in the Rue de la Paix. When he got there he found the shops closed. He had to resign himself to return to the boulevard, where he bought a little golden purse for ten louis. It was pretty, with its flexible close links. Before having it wrapped up he placed in it his twenty-five louis. Then he was surprised to see that it was close on nine o'clock. He jumped into a cab, told the man to go to the Madeleine, and got there five minutes late. As he approached the omnibus office he was alarmed at his emotion. At the first rendezvous he had ever kept, he had certainly been less agitated. He jumped out of the cab and sent it away.

By the open door he saw Anna. She had no hat on,

and was dressed, as the day before, very poorly. In spite of the cold she had on a bodice of rose-coloured calico. He felt ashamed to accost her before the people there. He was already making her a sign to follow him when he saw an old roué, a well-dressed gentleman, speak to her. She smiled, and seemed to reply pleasantly. George thought he had seen enough. He resolutely turned his back and hurried away. Before long he slackened his speed. Then, turning round, like a madman, he burst into the omnibus office, and ran to Anna. He was filled with rage. She got up quickly. He took off his hat, and stood uncovered in front of her. She held out her hand, and at the contact of her flesh he trembled. However, everybody was looking at them, astonished to see this man, so elegant in manners, and so polite to this pretty girl, who, evidently, was desperately poor.

"Put on your hat," she said. "Go in front, I will follow you."

He obeyed her. But in the street he had to turn round. It was stronger than he was. And he saw her, stood in front of the old man, who had just been speaking to her. The man nodded his head in sign of acquiescence, and handed Anna something which she put in her pocket. George felt his heart tighten. She came out. He walked by her side, taking her arm. Anxiety as regards the passers-by had left him.

" What did the old man say to thee ? "

" What 's it matter to thee ? "

He bent his head, looking at her. How pretty she was ! She had no corset on, her closely fitting garment clung to her figure, with its little marvellous breasts, and its round and well-shaped form. She walked with a steady step, her heels ringing on the pavement with little firm blows. She did not utter a word, but looked askance at him from the corner of her eye. They stepped in front of a decent looking house in the Place de la Madeleine. As he rang, he motioned to her. And in an altered voice, almost indistinct with emotion, he said to her :

" Another word—it is very serious—I beg of you never again to do to me what you did last night."

She laughed mockingly. And contemptuously, scornfully :

" What ? Toss thee off ? But, my kid, I shall do what amuses me. To me thou art nothing but a slave to whom I do just what I wish."

He did not know what to reply, and was so troubled that he could scarcely press the electric button.

III

A servant shewed them into a room. After having lit the eight candles which were on each side of the clock on the mantelpiece, she discreetly went out. Anna remained standing, a little embarrassed before all this luxury. She whispered:

"You do yourself well. It is very swell here. Is it your house?"

George smiled, happy at seeing the curiosity of a child.

"What do you think? Merely a short-time house."

She seemed surprised, and with regret in her voice: "I have never seen such beautiful things. But why isn't there a bed?"

"Because this is the parlour. The bed-room is there, behind that portière, with everything necessary for love-making. Shall I take you there?"

"No! Stay where thou art."

She drew aside the portière, and going in the bed-room, uttered cries of admiration. "There is a bidet!"

she called out joyfully. He heard the glouglou of water being poured out. Not waiting any longer, he went and raised the curtain, and had just time to catch sight of her, astride of the bidet, shewing her well-shaped legs, and vigorous backside. She cried out to him, irritatedly, "Wilt thou be off?" Such was the ascendancy which she already had over him, that he hastened to obey her. He cooled his toes in an easy chair until she came back. As she passed him, George tried to draw her to him. But she moved away from him, and went prying about all over the room. She felt at the curtains, stopped to touch the velvet-pile carpet, opened the piano, and tapped on it with a timid finger. And her every attitude shewed a supple and powerful grace. George kindled more and more. His desire gnawed him, brooking no delay. Anna sank into a fauteuil, on a very low seat, and sighed delightedly: "God, how nice it is here!" George could no longer restrain himself. Kneeling in front of her, he gave her the purse.

"Is it for me?" she asked, pleasantly.

"Whom do you wish it to be for?"

She took off the silk paper, opened the box, and drew out the purse, which shone with a yellow lustre, swollen with its twenty-five louis.

"Is it gold?" she asked, in an almost frightened voice.

"Of course! and its contents also are."

44

Anna opened the purse, took out a louis, which she made to flash, with a curious amused air, and burst out laughing. Spreading her knees open, she emptied the purse. A shower of gold fell into her lap. "How much is there?"—"Five hundred francs."—"Five hundred francs!" she gravely repeated. And suddenly her eyebrows contracted. "Are those good pieces?"—"If you have the least doubt I can ring and get them changed for banknotes."—"No. I prefer gold." She played with the purse. And all at once she again put on this severe air, this tone of commandment which disconcerted George, sharpening his lust. She handed him the purse.

"Go, and put that on the mantelpiece. Then go in the next room, and undress thyself. Keep nothing on thee, not even thy socks."

He threw a look on her, full of passion and gratitude. Doubtless, the moment of pleasure approached. He undressed himself in a few seconds, and slipping naked into the bed, he called, "Anna!"—"Eh, well? you are undressed? Come here!"

He got up, grumbling. What was it which still drew him to this whore? She could do nothing like other women. He returned into the parlour, and at his first step, remained immoveable, struck with admiration. She stood upright in front of the American stove, where anthracite was glowing, under a mica screen. She had kept on her little slippers, her stockings and her chemise, the tail of which she had raised, exposing her plump buttocks to the heat. And nothing was so lascivious as this slender figure in this gallant déshabillé. Superb arms, round and muscular, the triceps slightly projecting: the arms of a Spartan wrestler. A full throat, bold and plump. And George's looks wandered delightedly from the robust neck to the nervous legs. But the shoulders above all charmed him; sloping shoulders, delicate and gracile, without being thin. He had feared doubtful underclothing, and she appeared to him with tiny slippers, black silk open-work stockings fastened by mauve garters with bunches of ribands at their side, and a chemise of diaphanous cambric. She smiled pleasantly at him, and sat down in the easy chair.

"Come!" He sat beside her, mad with lust.

"Thou hast been nice. The purse was a delightful surprise. Here—take—" And she held out her lips.

He uttered a groan of joy. Rushing forward, he seized the kiss. And he seemed to cling for ever on her mouth. She took his upper lip between hers, sucked it sweetly, and her agile tongue slipped everywhere, cooling his palate with an icy freshness, and running torrents of flame through his veins. She drew back a little.

"Open thy mouth!"

46

And from above, bending her roguish hand, she let her saliva run.   He drank it greedily, uttering gurglings of pleasure.   But already she held it.   She had taken his prick fully in her hand.   Grasping it lightly, her fingers just touched the flesh.   She made them glide with a long slow movement, from the beginning of the testicles to the extremity of the gland.   And this touch, so light at the commencement, tightened.   By a slow and continued progression, she strained George's nerves to breaking point.   It was desire with all its anguishes, grievous and infinite passion.

He cried : "Anna !   My sainted Anna !   Have pity— Oh ! thy body, thy noble body !   Give it me !"

She did not reply, darting on him the sombre fire of her large velvety eyes.   He implored :

"Thy mouth !   Oh, thy mouth !.   Thy lips, so fresh ! so sweet !"

She commanded.

"Spend !"

"Yes ! yes ! a kiss ! for pity's sake !"

She filled his mouth with her tongue, and hurried the movement of her fingers.   He spent with pangs of pleasure, his entire body writhing convulsively.   And he rose up and stood stupidly at her side.

"Go and fetch me some water and a towel !"

He hastened, and brought her the basin.   She washed her hands, and went and sat in the easy-chair by the fire.

"Let us chat! You will reply truthfully. Besides, if you wished to lie, I should know it. You begin to know me, don't you? Are you married?"—"Yes."— "Do you love your wife? Does she love you?"—"I say! Wilt thou do me the pleasure of talking about something else?" She boxed his ears soundly. "First of all, go on thy knees. There, in front of me. And now, take care not to call me "thou" again! Reply now!"

He knelt humbly. She again took hold of his prick, and held it in her hand. He begged her: "Anna, come and make love!"—"I will see about that presently—Answer me!" He spoke in hiccoughs, stammering, "Yes, my wife loves me: I love her, also. Tenderly, as I love my children. But the flesh is dead."

"Madame thy wife is perhaps cold?"—"On the contrary, very warm. She always wants it."—"Is she pretty?"—"I have her portrait in my pocket. Would you like to see it?"—"Yes!" He returned with the photograph, and tried to lean over the back of the easy-chair. "Eh, what? go back where you were!" He docilely went again on his knees. She snatched the portrait from his hands, and again seized his prick "But thy wife is quite young?"—"Thirty-two years old."—"She does not look it. She is very pretty; she has not the air of a tart, like I have. Go and put this where you took it from." He returned, and at her gesture, went again to her feet. "And me, dost thou love me?"—"Madly!"—"Thou liest; you desire me, that's all. You perhaps hate me! I don't care! What is certain is that I hold you through your flesh, and that you fear me. I prefer that, it is more certain than love. Listen! the six louis which you gave me yesterday—I have bought these slippers, these stockings, this chemise. I had nothing left even to buy handkerchiefs with. You cannot however walk with me in this dress I have here, hidden behind this screen."

"I will buy you some costumes; but I will not walk out with you."

"Why?" she asked, and her fingers, motionless till then, moved like tentacles, fingering his standing prick. He shuddered under the rude caress, and was silent, again dazzled with the vertigo of desire. "Speak!"— "Because I do not wish to give pain to my wife, and I will not walk with——"—"With what? finish then." He remained silent. "Say the word! Bah! you dare not! I will say it for thee. You do not wish to be seen with whores. Isn't it so?" He protested with a gesture. "Lie down. There, at my feet. On your back: at full length."

He obeyed. She put her slippered foot on his mouth. Although she scarcely pressed on it, it seemed to him that he was supporting a mountain. With her open hand she placed his prick in the crease of her palm, pressed on it, and began shaking it by turning it rapidly. The stiff prick tossed madly, following the rapid impulsion of her hand. It was a bitter, infatuating sensation. George howled, crying for mercy.

He had to spend again.

"Get up! on your knees! you will come to-morrow in a cab, to the corner of the Faubourg du Temple and the Quai de Jemmapes, at the wine shop. I shall be there. You will take care to bring some money and we will go together to buy what I want. Is it agreed?"

"I will come," he murmured, quite tamed.

She tickled his nipples. Gently at first, then roughly. He struggled to get away. She struck him, again took his nipples and pinched them, pulled them and recommenced gently tickling them. Her hand descended. Her fingers pressed on his pubis, and wandered to his groin, where they pinched his testicles; and pulling some hairs out, she shewed them to him. He again had a cockstand. He started imploring her, he knelt down and licked her slippers, whilst with his trembling hands he caressed her calves. "Shall I never have thee?" he groaned. "Shall we never make love?"

"We will talk about that presently. To-day I intend to frig thee till the blood comes. Thou must feel my empire over thee. Thou must belong to me body and soul, so that thou wilt obey me blindly."

Everything she said to him entered into his brain like

points of fire. He felt that she spoke the truth, that he
was her humble and submissive slave, her thing, which
she could dispose of at her pleasure. The more she
humiliated him, the higher she grew in his eyes. A
strange curiosity, an unutterable pleasure, were mingled
with his terror. He wished she would be able to make
his blood spurt, yet he was afraid of it. But he felt his
head was empty, and his arms and legs seemed broken
at their joints. And all his nerves were vibrating. His
virility fled to his private parts, and strained towards
Anna. He cherished, whilst fearing, her redoubtable
yet gentle hand. She thrust him backwards. He fell at
her feet.

She took his prick in her full hand, her thumb and
index finger joined together, forming a ring too tight for
the gland to be able to pass through it. Then she
began to frig him roughly.

" Look what I am doing to thee," she said.

He raised his head, and was frightened. She fumbled
amongst her hair, and pulled out a large hair-pin, with
which she pricked his balls, without ceasing to frig him.
He sighed out a desperate complaint, and attempted a
last revolt.

" I will not spend ! "

" Spend ! I wish it ! "

The crystal of her voice was still vibrating when the
ejaculation seized him. He no longer stirred, but lay

exhausted and breathless. She pushed him with her foot.

"Get up! you haven't finished. Get up on your knees, and let us talk. You wanted to know what the old man at the omnibus office said to me. He said he had never seen as pretty a woman as I am. That I am intoxicating; that I have the proud and haughty air of an empress; that I have teeth which will crunch fortunes. And that I have but one word to say to have a furnished flat, a motor car, a horse and carriage. I asked him if it was to him that I must say this word. He replied, 'yes.' I promised to think it over, and asked his name. And there is his card on the mantel-piece. Tell me if you know who he is."

George scrutinized the card. "'Marquis de Cazzavoglio, Avenue Rembrandt.' An Italian!"—"Yes, he had an absurd accent. Do you know him?"—"By name. He is a big brewer."—"Is he rich?"—"He spends a great deal."—"Good! Now tell me: do you still want to make love?"—"You have exhausted me! I am used up," he groaned with a piteous air.

"Go on! You have still got spunk, and it shall come out, I promise you!—But you understand that if I have told you all this, it is because I want you to furnish a flat for me. You will do it—and it must be a dainty one; like this, but better!"

He did not reply, but was visibly annoyed.

"Hast thou heard me?" she insisted. "Yes. But what do you want me to reply? My head is swimming round. You have stupefied me."

"Very well! I am going to clear your thoughts. Turn round. There,—bend your head down, take your ankles in your hands. Open your legs."

He uttered a cry. She had thrust a finger in his backside, and she pressed on the prostate gland, crushing it. Instantly, he had a cockstand. She passed her other hand between his legs, and squeezing his prick, she bent it down, pulling it backwards and forwards with a movement as though she were milking it. It was quickly done At the end of a couple of minutes he discharged mournfully. He fell in front of her, letting his head drop on her knees.

"Anna! Anna! will you never have pity?"—"Perhaps! but all that I make thee endure excites me. Come and suck me off."

She threw off her chemise, appearing in her slender, splendid nakedness. She stretched herself along the couch. And George greedily attacked the dessert. The perfume immediately intoxicated him. And he went forward fervently, full of devotion for this radiant woman, the living incarnation, amongst all others, of pleasure. She sighed, pinched his ear, pulled his hair, and caressed his private parts. He sucked without ceasing, biting her. At last she spent, and he greedily sucked the cyprine. She got up:

" Hein ! you're proud of having made me spend ! I must recall to you that you are only a slave. I must humiliate you thoroughly. Suppose I shit in your mouth ? what do you say ? "

He believed it was a gross pleasantry. But already the crudity of the words sickened him.

" You are mad ! "

With a prompt movement she seized him by the balls, and squeezed them. The pain was atrocious. He cried out desperately, and when she let go, he fell, crushed, at her feet. Turning her back she stooped over his face. Thus he saw the whole of her, and under the weight of her look, he dare not move.

" Thou hast swallowed my spit, gobbled my spunk, now I am going to piss in thy mouth ! "

A bitter flood beat on his face, blinding him. He felt a salty and slightly bitter taste on his palate.

" Attention ! " she went on. " Here is the shit I told you of ! "

She dilated her eyes, and pressed her lips together in the effort. George thought she had the severe and dreaded look of a divinity. But he looked lower down. A rosy flush passed along the pearly whiteness of her buttocks. The fetid aroma spread itself. And the turd appeared. Terrible, superb ! It slowly came out of the enlarged hole, lengthening itself, threateningly. And it sprang forward with the supple movement of a snake. It pressed heavily on George's mouth. The smell was strong like the bouquet of a generous wine. His nostrils palpitated. He breathed heavily, and felt heartened.

Anna got up: "Don't move!" She took a newspaper, and put the turd in it. "Take the lather off thee." He washed himself with a lot of water, rubbing furiously, as if with rubbing the skin he thought he could remove the disgrace. She watched him doing it, smiling strangely and cruelly.

A corner of her lip was turned up showing a milky line of teeth.

"Hurry up! You're going to wipe my arse. What? you're looking for paper? Idiot! With your tongue, if you please. And see that you leave nothing. Lick!"

She bent down. With her legs a little open, she remained stooping, her hands resting on the arms of the easy-chair. Bending over her plump buttocks, George slipped his tongue into the pretty hole. A sweet and oily taste, a thick lusciousness tickled his palate. He licked zealously, and went on licking. But Anna pushed him away. "Enough! Go and rinse your mouth." He returned, so humble, so disconcerted. She was seated in the easy-chair; and naked, with her arms raised above her head, she offered herself in a ravishing pose. He began to cry. Tears ran from his eyes. And he did not think of restraining them. She seemed astonished. "What is it?"—"You are so beautiful, so desirable. And now it is finished! You will never love me! After such a proof of your contempt—"

"Stop it!" she said chaffingly. "Everything comes. Hope! Do I despise thee? Yes, I despise thee. Not more than the others. Every man who will love me, I shall dominate. Stop crying, or I shall be annoyed. Here! On your knees!"

He was in front of her. With the tips of her fingers she encircled the gland, and began to twitch his prick. The member speedily stiffened itself. She irritated it by learned spider touches. Her fingers fluttered as far as his anus. "Anna! Anna!" She got up, ordering, "Remain on thy knees. Creep to the easy-chair. Put thy cock on it."

Transversely, making a cross with his prick, she put her foot on it, clad in a dainty slipper. The prick was held between the sole of her foot and the cloth of the easy-chair. She moved her leg with a backwards and forwards movement, a vigorous rubbing. He implored her, and with his trembling hand, he caressed the murderous leg, carried away by its beauty. "Spend!"— "I cannot!"—"He says that he loves me, yet he cannot spend for me!"—"Oh, yes! Anna! Anna! Darling mistress, have pity on thy slave—Thy hand—thy dear hand, to my lips!" Without interrupting the action of her foot, she abandoned her hand to him. He kissed it frantically, ate it with caresses.

"Anna! Anna! Loved goddess! I am spending! For thee—for thee—"

The sperm sprang out underneath her sole. George panted. He had a little dry cough. Sweat pearled on his forehead, glueing his hair to his temples; and his eyes, circled with a livid stain, shone with a feverish brightness. Neuralgia darted through his brain, and his elbows ached frightfully.

"Shall we go away?"—"As I am not in a hurry, thou hast no need to be; and then we must continue our previous conversation. I want a furnished flat. You will arrange all that?"

He was silent.

"Is it yes or no?"—"You know well enough. The instant you command, what can I do? I can only obey."—"You say that, because I am here. But immediately I shall have left you, you will again try to revolt, although I know that the remembrance of me will be the strongest. But I wish it to be still more acute— If you are tired, lie down on the easy-chair."— "I am cold and hungry."—"So am I, I could willingly break a crust. Why didn't you think of bringing something?"—"It is easy to put that right; I have but to ring. They will bring us what we want. Some cold chicken, a pâté de foie gras, and a lobster." She clapped her hands joyously. " I would willingly eat all these. I would even drink something if it is good !"— " Would you like some champagne ?"—" Ring ! Ring !"

He ordered the supper through the door. In less than quarter of an hour it was brought. Whilst the table-cloth was being laid, they went in the other room to conceal their nakedness.—"Lie down !" — "And you ?"—"I will join you." A hope, a mad joy shone in his eyes. " Anna ! My dear mistress !" he murmured.

She was close to him, their bodies touching. His prick stood. He was taking her in his arms, when her hand stopped him. She had opened the lips of the meatus, and her thumb was touching the mucous membrane. She frigged him with little rapid shakings, with the continued shock of her hand against his stomach. George looked miserable and desperate; he did not even beg her not to, knowing her implacable. Although the servant had said the food was ready, she still went on frigging him.

" Darling mistress ! I cannot, there is nothing left !"— " If I have to frig thee till to-morrow morning, thou wilt spend !"

He exhausted himself with desperate efforts, the muscles of his neck and of his thighs stretched out. She went on frigging him, always with the same energetic movement.

" I will tear thy cock off, rather than leave it un-
finished. I want thy blood, and I will have it."—
"Wicked, wicked woman !"—"Spend !"—"Oh ! yes—
yes—"—" I wish it !"

His heart throbbed. She threw off the covering, and
pushing his head, forced him to look. The sperm came
out without any power, mingled with red points of blood,
and all the urethra was red, and bloody round its border.
He swooned away, closed his eyes, and lost conscious-
ness. When he came to himself again, he saw Anna
seated at his side, looking at him indifferently.

"Wilt thou eat anything?" He got up, groaning.
His entire body was twisted with cramp. And he
started devouring the food. "Eat !" she said. "Eat,
you have earned it. Do you know what time it is?
Look at the clock. It was half past nine when you
spent for the first time. It is now midnight. I have
made you discharge six times. That's not bad. When
I let you fuck me, you will be still keener. You don't
know what joys my body has for you"—"Anna !
Anna !"—"Eat, little one. Eat, and let us go."

She showed him an example, eating with the prowess
of a young healthy being whose vigour demands sus-
tenance. "You have a good appetite !"—"Dame !
When one has worked ! Admit that to make thee spend
six times in two hours and a half, one cannot be a
sluggard."—"You are very young?"—"Guess."—" It

59

is difficult. You have the face of a child. And you are made like a woman of twenty-five, who is a virgin."
—"I am seventeen years old!"—"And so—learned?"
—"Yes, my dear, so vicious! and some day I will tell thee all about it, so that thou wilt see how I have become so. Now I cannot, because I have got my mouth full of lobster."

He looked at her with a fervent admiration. The look of the lover who hopes. "Eat!" she said. And as he buried his nose in his plate, she cried out: "George!" He raised his head, and saw her darting on him her sombre look, this malicious look which always troubled him, and which never failed in its meaning. Annoyed, he threw his fork down. "How wicked you are!" She burst out laughing. "Eat!" But he was no longer hungry. His senses, grumbling, took away his fatigue. An idea came to him. Suppose he played a trick on her? He pressed her to take more champagne. But she drank moderately. He insisted. "You want to make me drunk? Imbecile, triple idiot! You don't know what will happen to you. You would pass a bad quarter of an hour. I would make you spend till I made you discharge your bowels. I would split up the mattress in order to have them." He turned pale. And terror again excited him.

"How good you would be if you stayed with me. Suppose we pass the night here."—"A great deal you could do!"—"I may be dead, but, to have you, I would have a resurrection."—"Fool! Little fool! Come and let us go! Or else—" A gesture completed her phrase. She made a movement as though she were frigging him. He threw down his serviette and fled into the next room, and hastened to dress himself, pursued by the vibrations of her laughter. Arm in arm, they went from the house. On the boulevard, the people were coming out of the theatres, and the street was crowded. People turned round to look with curiosity at this ill-matched couple; this tall fine girl, badly dressed, on the arm of a gentleman. But George, entirely occupied by Anna, did not care a straw about the passers-by. He hailed a cab. "Must I pay the cabman and go away? Or will you permit me to come with you?" She hesitated a second. "Come!"

IV

JOYFULLY, George leapt into the cab. "Where will you go?"—"Cité Popincourt." Without any enthusiasm the cabman started his horse on this interminable journey. George took Anna's hand, and stroked it gently. She remained pensive. Occasionally, under an electric globe, he saw her delicate profile, her big brown eyes shining like gems. Then everything again went into shadow. But fatigue had made keener the strange odour which her skin distilled.

"You 're not cold?"—"Never!"

However he took off his overcoat, and insisted on covering her with it. She let him do so, and they were again silent. Before a large café concert some women were accosting men. Anna, amused, bent out of the window.

"Aren't they stupid? I didn't get hold of thee like that, did I?"—"First of all, they have neither your youth nor your beauty; and then, there are few men who would let themselves do as I did."—"You think

62

so? You believe that an energetic man would be different? No! It is because women are so easy-going."—"There are very few who have your character; and at your age it is marvellous!"

"Why should I not tell you the circumstances? Although already it is full of events, my life can be told in a few words. My father was a hawker; greedy and not a drinker, so that when he died he left a little hoard behind him. I was then seven years old. He had not been underground six months when my mother went to live with a hair-dresser. The rascal was a widower with one daughter. He began by taking our money. And then all the sweetmeats were for his little one, and all the thumps for me. When my mother interfered, if she risked a word, she also felt the weight of his fist, and was doubled up at once, as limp as a glove. I consoled myself by running loose with the neighbours' children. We had mad parties; hardly any girls, but all the wicked lads of the neighbourhood. You should have seen how I handled them. If there was one who resisted, or wanted to take liberties which displeased me, I quickly had his trousers open. Immediately I had his prick in my hand, it stood. I frigged him till he cried for mercy. More than one of them, since become a famous bully, the terror of his neighbourhood, have I tamed like this. When I was fourteen years old, I was as tall as I am now, and my stepfather got fond of me.

The best bits were for me, the others could whistle for them. One night, as I was sleeping quietly, the cold woke me up. A man in his nightshirt had thrown off the counterpane, and had already put his foot in the bed. I cried out, and he put his hand on my mouth, swearing that he would kill me. But as he was going to take me, I caught hold of him by the balls, and then— I squeezed hard. He howled! And then there was nothing more. Good-night. Snuffed out like a candle. I didn't leave hold. But they had heard him cry out. My mother ran in with some neighbours. It was quite a business to tear him from my hands, and then to make him open his eyes again. He was ill for weeks, and even now he is not yet cured of his fear. When he sees me coming, he hides himself. My mother apprenticed me to a big shoe-maker of la Villette. Do you know what I did there? For ten hours with a hammer and a steel anvil I nailed soles on ; and I earned fifteen pence a day. The workmen prowled after me and gentlemen in the street made overtures to me. They disgusted me, and I told them so. One evening, as I was coming from work, very tired, an old man looked at me. He turned round and followed me. He was not at all like the others, who always put on lordly airs. He scarcely dared look at me, and he said : " Mademoiselle, I beg you, will you permit me to say a word to you?" I replied to him : " A word? It is I who will say it to you: Shit!" That went through him like a shock. Tears came to his eyes, his hands trembled, and he said: "Alas! Mademoiselle, if you do not deign to listen to me, in leaving you I shall lose the happiness of my entire life." I replied to him, "Alright! speak! But none of your jokes!" Whereon, he began by handing me five francs. He excused himself for not being rich, otherwise he would have given me much more, and he said that I deserved a fortune; and he added that if he could come every evening to conduct me to the end of my way, he would give me five francs each time. I thought I had to deal with a fool; but what did I risk? I told him that he would never have me in return for his money. He said that if one day, no matter when, even at the end of a year, I would give him my hand to kiss, he would go on his knees and believe himself well paid. He came every day, during an entire month, before I allowed him to kiss my hand. Then he wept. He informed me that he had always sought for, and had never found a woman such as I was. That I was made to trample on mankind, stretched at my feet. And that he preferred to toss himself off every night, whilst thinking of me, rather than to sleep with the smartest cocotte in Paris. I said nothing at the moment. But as he was saying good-day, I wished to see his lodging. He danced in the street, joy made him so mad. We arrived there, and on the way he bought some foie gras, some fried potatoes, and some oranges, and he went on his knees to wait on me. He asked nothing from me; he did not even touch my dress. I was already on the landing, going away, when I turned back abruptly, and without saying a word to him, I unbuttoned him and tossed him off. You know how to spend? Nothing like this man! And what a charming man! He was so intellectual, such a good talker, and had the manners of a gentleman. "If I had only known you earlier!" said he. "I was rich—I ruined myself for a woman whom I imagined was the being which you really are. With your seductive way and force of character, you will dominate over men. At the bottom, man is a filthy beast. Cruel with the weak, cowardly with the strong. Woman can tame man like a tiger. By masturbating him. Nothing enslaves him more. But there are few women; almost all are merely females. They do not know how to profit by the man's desire, so as to enchain him for ever. Satiety arrives, and the woman becomes the servant. Man is irresolute, and when woman shows him her power, her grovels at her feet; the more she humiliates him the better she dominates him." Poor old man! He took my maidenhead! With what care, what precautions! If all husbands acted in this manner, there would be few cuckolds. I profited by his lessons— but he is dead now. He died begging my pardon for not being able to leave me a fortune. Depriving him-self of everything, he had paid in advance two years' rent for his room, and the receipt was in my name. My stepfather hid himself when I went back, and my mother treated me badly, so I lived in the old man's room. The ponces of the neighbourhood tried to make a strumpet of me, but it didn't come off. And then afterwards I myself wanted to become one. As I hadn't even enough to buy a hat with, I thought I would try first on the faubourg du Temple, where smart men seldom pass. You were my first catch — and there's my history!"

George, whilst listening to her, had felt various senti-ments. He was indignant against her mother, he cursed her stepfather, and pitied the child's misery. Far from being jealous, he had a feeling of affection towards the old gentleman, who had also loved her, and who had been, like he was, her slave.

The cab stopped. "Anna!"—"Eh, well?"—"You are leaving me? You do not wish to stop with me!"—"To-morrow! Keep the cab to go home with, and go to sleep." She gave him her hand to kiss, and went away. He followed her slender silhouette with his eyes. "Rue Lesueur!"—"Again at the other end of Paris," grumbled the cabman.

George slept like lead. When he got on his feet, at ten o'clock next morning, he was overwhelmed when he thought of all that he had to do before meeting his mistress. Assisting at Anna's transformation was a banquet for his eyes. She carried her toilet with an elegance which equalled the perfection of her shape and the distinction which her imperiousness gave to her. George noticed that not only men but also women turned to look at her, with that look which they all have when they are envious of one of their own sex. Anna passed by indifferently, disdainful both of homage and of envy.

" And when do you wish to be happy?"—" At once ! " George replied. " Have you got the keys of the flat ? Is the furniture there?"—" Everything is ready ! Only I have not dared definitely to decide on anything without your consent."—" Where is it?"—" Avenue Mac-Mahon, near l' Étoile, on the first floor, fronting the street. Drawing and dining-rooms, bed-room, large cabinet de toilette, bath-room, kitchen, and servant's bed-room. It is a pleasant place, with plenty of air and light."—"And the furniture?"—" The drawing-room in Empire style, mahogany and green damask embroidered with yellow bees; a gilt bronze clock; an aulétride which would please a philosopher. The bed-room in walnut, Louis XV style, figured silk with white and heliotrope stripes, mauve flowerets on a white ground, and white on a mauve ground. The dining-room in modern style, green beechwood french-polished."

"I don't understand much about what you tell me. I have still a great deal to learn. However it seems to be better than having a furnished flat. But how have you managed it? How have you found the time in which to pick and choose?" — "From ten to two o'clock."—"And you've not lunched?"—"I've had a bite of lunch in the cab."—"But how will you manage to have everything ready for this evening? Do you know that it is already six o'clock?"—"The upholsterers await your orders. Let us go and see the flat, shall we? If it suits you, I will pay and telephone to the upholsterer, and to the furniture dealer. We will go to dinner and then to the theatre, and about midnight everything will be ready."

"Let us go!" she said, delightedly. But she did not wish to get out of the cab. "I will see everything when it is in its place. As for the house, it has a good appearance. You have chosen well."

They went to dine. George could not tire of admiring her. With her tall figure and her imperious ways, she had truly a grand manner, and under the big hat boldly perched on her head, her face was as alluring as possible. Still, George had to acknowledge that without a hat she was even more seductive, her beauty stood out better. She had perfect manners, and held herself very correctly. However, after the soup, she turned towards the large glass behind her, and whilst admiring herself in it, began making faces at herself. She wrinkled her eyes, and then widely opening them, she put on her inviting glances. Opening her lips, she uncovered her teeth, going through a strange and expressive miming which a woman less pretty than herself dared not have attempted. George, whose excitement had been continually increasing since the first instant he had met her, experienced a fresh rush of desire. She saw in the mirror his congested face, and his humid eyes imploring her. She still had her cruel smile, and turning towards him she put her foot on his, pressing on the nail most painfully. He had to submit to this pain until the dessert.

Afterwards, they hurried, fearing to be late for the theatre. She was as delighted as a girl from the country. All through the play she imitated the performers. He would have been puzzled to say what it was they played, so obstinately was he gazing at her, so much was he enraptured with the expressions of her face according to the incidents of the play. They chatted during the entr' actes. But in the very middle of a phrase he began to stammer, as with a furtive gesture her hand grazed him. At last this delicious martyrdom came to an end. They were in the cab, and he had already given the address to the cabman, when she spoke of supper.

"Or rather, go and buy what you can. We will sup

at my place."—"I have seen to that. The table is laid ready, waiting for us."—"Thou art a thoughtful slave, and I adore thee!"

Her supple and warm body weighed on him, pressing him against the side of the vehicle. Her wandering hands caressed him everywhere: on his loins, on his chest, along his neck, and as though in a dream, they lightly skimmed over his parts: an ephemeral and light touch.

"Anna! Anna! Enough, I pray you! You will make me spend!"—"No! I don't want to. Thou art going to by-bye in thy corner, I in mine."

They arrived. The staircase with its steps cut in white marble enchanted her. She clapped her hands in front of the Japanese vases in the dining-room, the confusion of green plants, and the table service of Sevres with the facetted cut glass, and smiled brightly when she noticed the drawing-room clock, a female flute-player seated on the back of a stooping oldster, a philosopher whom one recognized as such by his attributes,—his long beard and the roll of papyrus with which his hand was encumbered. But in front of the wardrobe with glass doors, an enormous piece of furniture, she stamped her feet with joy. A mad laugh, an hysterical laugh, shook her. With a turn of her hand her clothes were scattered on the pillow of an easy-chair. And in her corset, with a little silk petticoat, she was superb with

her wasp's waist, her bust thrown forward, her Diana-
like arms, before this large bevelled mirror which re-
flected the prettiness of her mischievous head. She
arched herself on her supple thighs, swelled out her
graceful and robust neck, and looked down on herself
admiringly. At her side, George, sunk on his knees,
was licking her shoes.

"Come and eat the nice things which I saw in the
dining-room, this is better than polishing my shoes."
But he implored her, grovelling in front of her; and his
desire so abolished all his faculties that he could no
longer find words. He repeated her name in a litany,
with an expressive fervour: "Anna! Anna! Anna!"

"What! Thou art so pressed? Wait, I will calm
thee!"—"Oh!" said he, retreating from her.

She laughed heartily.

"Coward! Are you then so frightened of being
tossed off. But you need it, my child. With your excitement, you would spend before you got inside me.
Does my hand frighten you? Well! I swear to you
that it shall not touch your precious cock! Come!"

He approached her, full of anguish. What was she
going to do to him now? She unbuttoned him, dropped
his trousers, and pulled up his shirt. "Look! look in
the mirror!" He saw himself, with his member, swollen,
enormous, at the side of this beautiful girl who was
working at him.

74

She had put her hand on his belly, amongst the hair, and the tip of her middle finger pressed strongly on the pubis, just at the extremity of the penis. She squeezed and rubbed him gently, her fingers scarcely touching him, as light as the footfalls of an insect. But the middle finger persisted in its terrible pressure, and the prick tossed about distractedly.

"You see, I am tossing you off, without touching your cock."

He repeated her name in a doleful voice, and spent abruptly. A jet of sperm sprang as far as the cornice. From that time he was gay, and a charming companion. But immediately she fixed him with her sombre look, he became absent-minded, and began to stammer. He had also another subject of terror. She had undressed herself, and had ordered him to strip stark naked, but she herself had kept on her shoes and stockings. Was she going to send him away, immediately afterwards?

She lay down on the bed. With one bound he was upon her. So anxious was he that he was clumsy. She took his flanks between her nervous thighs, and closed on him tightly, with the grip of a vice. Then she juggled with him, alternately drawing him to, and pushing him from, the coveted goal.

With tears in his voice, he protested: "Anna! Anna! What! So near happiness, and I shall not have you."

She put her fingers to her mouth, and wetting them,

took his prick, and guided it. " You are very big and
I am quite tiny. Don't move." He obeyed, and as
the vagina dilated he gained ground. He seemed to
be gliding into a furnace; flames ran through his veins,
and mounted to his brain.

" Oh ! Anna ! Anna !"—" What more do you want ?
You are so excited that you will do no good at all.
Stay quiet, and let me do it."

She gave him her lips, and their tongues mingled.
Her powerful croup then set in motion. A quivering
of the buttocks, an horizontal movement of the belly,
and she made him feel an acute spasm. He fell exhausted at her side, and gratefully kissed her hand.
She went into the cabinet de toilette. " Feel in the commode with the marble top, the large commode with the
swelling front, and you will find the night linen." She
smiled, enraptured and surprized..

"Good ! you shall have your reward. Go to sleep
and regain your strength. Take care not to move
about in the bed. Sleep—" But already hope was exciting him. " And you have not even got an erection !"
she observed, whilst shaking disgustedly his flabby and
drooping prick. " If you wished?"—" No ! Sleep !
I am putting out the lamp."

He scarcely slept, being too agitated by his remem-
brances, and hope and fear. However, towards morning he fell into a heavy stupor. When he woke up, by

the pale light of day which filtered through the curtains he saw her sleeping at his side, her arms folded above her head, her haughty neck heaving with the movements of her bosom. How pretty she was! The gray dawn could not tarnish her brightness. He lost himself in veneration, contemplating her. She woke up with the morning's thickness of speech, the broad dialect of the country girl.

"Shit! Breakfast? You hav'n't thought about it?"

"Oh, yes! What does Madame desire? Chocolate or café au lait?"—"Goose! chocolate and some rolls!"

He pressed an electric button, and someone knocked at the door. Speedily a woman came, who bore the chocolate smoking hot on a lacquer tray. They breakfasted in bed. He looked at her continually, his eyes saying so clearly he counted on her to work a miracle that she burst out laughing.

"Poor puss! You want to make love and you cannot get an erection! Don't worry yourself. Drink your chocolate. Eat some brioches; and in a short time you will see."

As a matter of fact, he did see. He had to get out of bed and stretch himself on the ground on his back, with his legs open and his knees raised. She made a lather of soap, and covered her hands with it as far as her wrists. She got astride of him, with her face turned towards his feet; and straddled across him with her backside on his face.

"You are going to suck me, and put your tongue up my arse-hole. Hurry up!"

He licked. She took his prick in her right hand which was covered with lather, rubbed forcibly, and her left hand, descending lower, attacked his behind. He had an erection. Without leaving him, she slipped a little towards his feet, and with a prompt movement she lodged his prick in her cunt, whilst her moistened finger continued pushing in his anus without ceasing. He saw her darkened neck, her large and satiny back, and above it her slender waist, and her enormous backside frisking about, resembling a gluttonous and ferocious beast, an implacable beast which sucked to the very marrow, and which one was unable to resist. He spent as he had never spent before. This acme of fatigue with this beautiful girl so ardently desired was pleasure in such an intensity that it consisted of nothing but suffering.

V

"You must get off, and go home. To-night at seven o'clock you will call for me, we will dine at a restaurant, and you will take me to a theatre. But there is something wanting here."—"What is it?"—"My sceptre." —"What do you mean?"—"You must bring me a whip, I want one which is flexible and strong and solid, and yet tiny and pretty."—"But, you are describing yourself."—"Quite so. And when you behave badly, your backside will find the resemblance stronger."

"Are you dissatisfied with me?"—"No! But your docility won't last. You will always have some inclination to rebel. Oh! I am not afraid! I know how to tame you. But, my child, you don't seem to understand what a mistress is. For instance: your child, your favourite daughter, might be dying and I should send you to the Bastille to get me a twopenny trinket. You would go, you would obey me! Do you understand?"—"Yes!" he murmured, so pale and troubled that he could scarcely breathe. "And you will do

77

everything that I wish?"—"Everything, darling mistress! Everything! I swear it to you!"—"We shall see. Don't forget the whip!"

He did not forget it. His first business was to get it at the place where Anna had sent him to. Then he went home. His wife greeted him without a word of reproach. But he was alarmed to see how haggard she looked, with hanging cheeks and drawn features. And her beautiful eyes were discoloured, and swimming in tears which she would not let flow in his presence. His daughters were silent, timid, and full of uneasiness. Embarrassed, he felt his anger fermenting, when he opened his arms to his wife. She let herself fall in them, weeping.

"My George! My George is with me!"

"What now? Here's a fine story. Then—must I give up my candidature; renounce everything?"

She smiled a bitter smile, impressed with sadness. She did not tell him that the members of his committee had sent to ask him to join them as speedily as possible. Suddenly she began to cough. A dry and violent cough which convulsed her entire body, shook her head from side to side dolefully. He was alarmed, and said in a pitying voice: "What is the matter?"—"Oh, nothing. A cold."—"You must see the doctor."—"Let it alone, it will go as it came."

He was already at the telephone. But he had to

hurry away to his office, to give instructions to his clerk who was doubtless puzzled by his absence. He came back for lunch.

" And the doctor ? "—" He was not at home, but they will send him here to-night. Are you going out ? "—" I must ! It is annoying, I should so much have liked to have met the doctor. But you understand—" he stammered.

She understood only too well. So clear was her comprehension that she had to get up, press her handkerchief against her mouth to stifle her sobs, and to take refuge in the next room, where she burst into tears.

He did not know what to do, being more annoyed than sincerely distressed. Certainly, he would have done everything for his wife. But he recalled each word: " If your daughter, your favourite, were dying and I should send you to the Bastille to get me a trinket, you would go, you would obey me ! " Oh, yes ! to obey Anna was his first duty. Besides, could he do otherwise ? the brief minutes already seemed to him immense.

At last the time came. Anna unpacked the whip, and made it whistle through the air ! " It is perfect ! " During the entire evening she showed herself affectionate, thankful for his attentions, resembling other women in every manner. Disdaining a cab she took the omnibus, and in spite of the cold she climbed on to the top. Even when they came out of the theatre, as he was insisting on hailing a cab, she threatened him with her finger. "No! I want to walk." They went back on foot, the longest way round. She went along the great boulevards, and the Champs-Élysees, and it was only when they reached the Étoile that she deigned to explain: "Do you see, my little one, in a cab, pressed close to me, you would get too much of an erection. You must sleep to be ready for the attack. I have exhausted you too much. Come to-morrow morning, at nine o'clock!"

He tried to soften her. But she had sworn not to treat him badly, and in her insinuating, even voice she repeated: "No! Nothing to-day. And you will be content with having obeyed me."

This word decided him. To obey her! Was not this his duty? So sweet a duty that it bore in itself its recompense. However, when they arrived at her door, he again implored her. "If you knew how I suffer! be good—let me come upstairs an instant with you—one minute—a poor little minute, and then I will be off!"

She had already rung. "To-morrow!" The open door closed on him: she had disappeared. He remained on the footpath, his eyes raised towards her windows, through which a light shone. He did not even see her shadow. The next day a plump soubrette, with dimples everywhere, opened the door for him. "Madame awaits Monsieur!" She showed him into the cabinet de toilette, and he heard the sonorous voice of Anna from the bath-room. "What art thou waiting for? Come here." She was in the vase of crystal, shaped like the hinged inside of a large shell. On all fours, she raised high her siren croup. In the glaucous water the play of reflections quivered, showing prismatically the pearl of her body, and drops from the points of her breasts shone iridiscently in rose drops of water. The light flickered, mobile, glinting with its flashes, and she seemed to frolic in a wave of precious stones. Across the stained-glass window, filtering through the bamboo and glass-bead curtains, a jet of brightness shone on her forehead like an aureole. And thus, hieratic, she recalled the image of Cypris, Venus Anadyomene, sprung from the wave. He approached her, so ravished that he had no words.

"Undress thyself, and come in with me." He entered the bath, prick on end. She splashed water over his head, and pinched him, laughing at his scared face. Raising herself a little, she pushed George deeper in the bath, and turning round, insinuated one of her legs between those of the man; then, taking his prick, she thrust it right up her cunt with one push.

"And now don't move! The least movement of my buttocks, and the movement of the water, will be sufficient. I warn you not to move!" He acted on her suggestion, and in spite of his ardour and the impetu-

81

osity of his desire, he remained still. A delicious torpor, with this scarcely noticeable balancing, this rhythmic cradling, led him gently towards the orgasm.

"Oh—Anna! Anna!" She also was swooning. "Is it good, my doggy?" He kissed her hands. "How sweet and calming it was! Just now I longed for you, but now I love you!"—"You think so?" she said, with her wicked smile. "Well, so much the better!"

She got out of the bath, and dried herself, whilst George devoutly admired her supple and powerful form.

"I give thee two minutes to get dressed," she cried to him. "After which there will be no longer anything to eat." He hurried, clumsily, and at last found himself at table with her. She forced the conversation, laughing at the sallies which she provoked. During a break in the conversation, he inconsiderately enquired, imitating a clown: "What are we going to do to-night?"—"Thou wilt stay at home."—"And you?"—"Thou art very curious! however, for once I will tell thee. To-night I am going to have a turn round Belleville. There is no reason, because I am in funds now, for me to forsake my comrades who knew me when I was down on my luck."—"But it is dangerous—and quite alone in evening dress!"

She laughed: "At Belleville, old chap, there is no one who would venture anything ill against Nana the fricatrice—and who tells thee that I shall go in grand tralala? Besides, I could flaunt myself at the 'Nouveau Siècle' with the Crown diamonds, and no one would say to me anything but what I wished to hear."

He looked at her, startled. Did she speak seriously? He was forced to believe so. She again put on her uncouth country accent: " Well! When you've finished staring at me! How stupid you look! No, really! Take your grand airs to your wife. And much pleasure for you at home. You know I am not keeping you."

He got up, and with a stiff gesture he took his hat, and bowed ceremoniously without a word whilst she was swollen with laughter. In the street he remembered the doctor, who had certainly that evening been to see his wife.

" I hope that she has only got bronchitis," said the doctor. " But if what I fear is true it will be terrible. Is there consumption in her family?"—"Not that I know of! You frighten me!"—"Be a man! You are rich, you can give her every care and distraction. Above all, see that she is ignorant of her complaint, and that she has no reason for unhappiness. Don't cross her in the slightest thing, but look after her and see that everyone round her also does so."

" No reason for unhappiness!" thought George as he went out. " Happily, I have finished with Anna! Thoroughly finished! There was a stupidity which cost me dearly. But it is not my money which I regret.

Sapristi!" (he cried, so loudly that the passers-by turned round) "What do I regret then? Certainly not the filthy actions of that whore!"

Although during the entire day he was nervous, he took great care of his wife, and had an unquiet solicitude after her welfare. She asked nothing better than to be blinded; happy at feeling her loved George near to her. And she pretended to have guessed nothing. What good was there in thinking of the past, when the present was so happy! But after dinner, George wandered about and could not sit still. He looked at his watch every instant, and though ready to go out, he came back and sat down in the corner of the fireplace.

"What is it? Have you any business on?"—"I should so much have liked to stay with thee. What a pleasant evening we would all have passed together. Bah! To the devil with this candidature, I shall stop here!"—"Not at all! Not at all! Go! I don't ask all your time from you. But you formerly spoilt me so much, that to abandon me completely would be too cruel!"

Poor woman! What should he do? No, decidedly, the best thing to do was to put on his slippers, and to dance his girls on his knee whilst telling them stories.

"You are not going? Go! I don't want you to regret it to-morrow."

He kissed her feverishly and went out. He went in search of the other one. Of the other one whom he did not love, whom he did not even desire any longer, but with whom he wished to disgust himself yet more, the better to cure himself. At the Place de la République he dismissed his cabman, and climbed on foot the faubourg du Temple and the rue de Belleville. He could see her nowhere, but he remembered that she had spoken of the " Nouveau Siècle." He asked his way, and was told that it was a café-concert on the boulevard de Ménilmontant, quite near Père-Lachaise. He ran there, as if he were afraid of arriving too late, of finding the establishment closed. Yet it was only nine o'clock. A single glance sufficed to assure him that she was not there. But as he was going out, he passed round a group of tables, and heard a bully say to his whore : " And la belle Nana, one never sees her now. Is she at Saint-Lago[1]?"

George sat down so as not to lose a word.

" Do you miss her?" replied the woman nastily. " Eh well, old chap, if you wish to keep her you are too late. It appears that she has found a mash. A smart fellow ! She's in gold and laces. There's a girl who's got luck!"—"You must be just. She's a fine looking girl, and not stupid !"—"There are others !"— " No! One must speak the truth. There are not others—God's name ! There's not a bloke in Pantruche who would not leave his trull to go with Nana,

[1] A slang term for the prostitutes' prison in Paris.

85

if she wanted him. At the end of ends one finishes with being disgusted with all these cows who daren't even go for a man when he puts his toe in their arse without really knowing why."—" Don't snivel!" growled the woman. "You will see your Nana. She'll be here shortly with Charlot the Wrestler. Big Mélie told me so."

George knocked on the table and ordered a warm wine. The room filled little by little. George saw people glancing under their eyelashes at him, the habitués of the place, wondering whom this well-dressed gentleman could be. However the numbers of the programme went on, until he saw her enter on the arm of Charlot the Wrestler. She was dressed poorly, in the rags which he had made her cease wearing.

She also had seen him. Under the arched bow of her eyebrows sprang an irritated glare. George, struck to the heart, and very pale, bent his head down.

Already she did not seem to think any more about him but turned to her lover, the "cock" of the quartier, with whom she was laughing whilst drinking a bottle of good wine. But her too strident laugh sounded false and reached George like a bravado and a menace. Anger growled in him. He asked himself if he ought not to go to them, and smash his glass on the wrestler's face. Evidently, this colossal big-belly did not know how to box, and as a rule wrestlers are afraid of a blow from a man's fist. Besides, if the knife joined the party, had he not his revolver? He stiffened his muscles, and felt that he could count on them. And he asked himself wherefore all these reflections? Formerly he had been much prompter in action. Had Anna's hand so depressed him then?

He got up, but began to tremble when he perceived her standing in front of him, with a tranquil and indifferent air. Her mouth was even smiling, but her eyes were hard and wicked. Her voice hissed, cuttingly : " I have to speak to thee ! Come !" He bent his head. and could not reply, stifled by the blood which flowed to his heart. He felt it beat fast and furiously. He sat down again, motioning to her a chair at his side.

She frowned, and repeated : " Come ! "

Already he was standing. And he followed her. It seemed to him that he was bound by an invisible thread whose ends she held.

Still, none of the people around seemed to take any notice of him. An affectation of not looking at him, which proved how much they were interested in the scene.

They were on the boulevard. She did not stop, but continued to walk, without appearing to care whether he followed her or not. He could not prevent himself admiring her vigour and her beauty. In her garments of a street-walker she had a strange seduction, brutal, and more sensual perhaps than in her fine attire. And, with her tall figure held erect, she walked with a firm and decided step which rang clear on the pavement.

But her silence alarmed George. He wished to take her arm. She drew it from him with a heavy blow

" Anna, you wish to speak to me ? "—" When it pleases me to, I suppose ? "

They walked on and he continued : " Anna, don't be cross ! listen to me—I beg of you—if you knew—I was so worried. I imagined a host of things—then, I went in search of you—and yet I should so much have loved to have stayed with my wife, to have looked after her. She coughs dreadfully, and the doctor is very uneasy ! "

She continued walking in silence, with an indifferent air to what he was saying. However, in the gloom, her little teeth shone. White and sharp. Her wicked smile curled up her lip, ironical and cruel. She took the rue de Panoyaux, and turning to the right she entered the impasse of the same name. The place was sinister. There was no one in this obscure and narrow place. They passed a gas-lamp, and further on, in a corner full of shadow, she stopped.

"So ! you permit yourself to spy on me ? "

She struck him with the full force of her arm. He cried pathetically : " Pardon ! Darling ! Pardon ! "— " It's not that I 'm annoyed at seeing you. You arrive at the right time. Give me your money—hurry up!"

"No! Not now! Not here! No, I don't wish to."

She unbuttoned him, and pushing her finger in his behind she poked up and down without any consideration. "Oh, là, là! Oh, là, là!" he cried, distractedly. "Will you shut up? Imbecile! The next thing you'll do is to call the 'tecs." With her free hand she ransacked his pockets, emptied them and took everything.

"On your knees now! And stick out your backside. Ah! if I had my whip this would be the time to give it a treat!" She kicked him thoroughly. The toe of her slipper went straight between his buttocks with all the vigour of a nervous and muscular leg. He groaned and writhed under the pain mixed with pleasure.

"Get up!"—"Yes! darling mistress! Yes! Pity!"— "You'll see about that!"

She wrapped his shirt round his prick, and seizing the whole with her hand she frigged him roughly. The linen rubbed against the delicate skin. "Oh! Anna! Anna! Mercy!"—"Spend, straight off! I wish it!"

He spent, reeling. An atrocious sensation, an exasperated delight, which the tenacious fingers of the girl prolonged until it became agony. And he remained there, stood in front of her, stupefied, tottering, his legs broken by the too rapid succession of the spasm of his discharge.

"Here are forty sous for you. You will take a cab

to the boulevard. There is a station quite close to the rue Oberkampf. You will go home. And the day after to-morrow—you hear me, the day after to-morrow, you will come to my place at mid-day."

"To-morrow—to-morrow, won't you? Be good!"

"Shit!"

She had already gone. He ran after her. "Anna! Anna! Don't leave me like this! A kiss—for pity's sake, a kiss! Your sweet lips—"

She stopped and penetrated him with her sombre look, her wonderful look of desire and love. Her velvety eyes sank into whirlpools of voluptuousness in which George's reason lost itself. And brusquely turning round she pulled up her clothes with both hands, and showed him her marvellous arse, her tight backside with its rebounding buttocks.

"Here! Kiss my arse! This happens alright. When I go into society I don't wear drawers!"

He knelt down in the gutter, and caressing her slim and nervous calves with his hands, he licked. "You will make me shit! Swallow this fart whilst waiting or better things!"

She farted. A little short crepitation. He shuddered, and with closed eyes, he breathed it in.

She had already gone. Her slim silhouette disappeared round the street-corner. Her firm step hammered the uneven pavement with little sonorous blows. The trilling of her strident and mocking laughter rang through the night.   On the boulevard, in the cab which was taking him homewards, George began to weep: " My wife ! my poor children ! "   And then, in a sudden re-action, in a burst of ardent adoration, he repeated in a litany the name of his mistress.

VI

ALL the day George surrounded his wife with an unquiet solicitude. From what he regarded as a renouncement, a sacrifice, he felt a joy which was full of bitterness. The illusion melted away in the evening, and he was agitated by a fever, an anguish which thrust him into the street. He went out with a hurried and rapid step, the blood mounting to his temples, and tingling in his ears. When he found himself at the Arc de Triomphe, the thought that he was again going to disobey her filled him with terror. He saw the house in the Avenue Mac-Mahon had its windows lit up, but that did not prove that Anna was at home. He would have liked to have walked up and down, and wait for her. To see her for an instant, he did not ask more. But if she perceived him, what would she say? He grew afraid, and hastened to return home. His affectionate devotion to his wife ended, and he was morose the whole evening, absorbed in an erotic imagination, a haunting full of terror and desire.

The critical moment came. "What have I done that you persist in sleeping apart from me? George! my George! return to me—" Taken unexpectedly, he became brutal. "Don't you see? After ten years of married life, it is no longer a pleasure!" In order to conceal a storm of tears, she again had to leave the room.

When mid-day struck, George, quivering with doubt and hope, reached Anna's flat. She received him in a ravishing costume. A tailor-made and figured woollen robe, which fitted her immaculately.

"To lunch!" she cried joyfully.

Before her good humour his gloom unbent. But he grew miserable again immediately he heard her say, "And how is thy wife?"—"Well, very well."—"Ah! so much the better!"

The phrase shocked him, but above all the tone. She did not seem to notice his discontent, and said:

"We are going to the races!"

At once he became annoyed and uneasy. He wished he was somewhere else. His bad temper was noticeable, but she persisted in ignoring it, and remained gay and full of spirits. She had never been to the races, and asked him, curiously, for particulars. When the servant brought the coffee, she told her they would take it in the bed-room. She placed herself in the front of the mirror. With the desire of dressing a little horsey,

93

she put on an astrakhan toque, decorated with a heron's feather, whilst George buttoned her boots : with trembling hands he did it so clumsily that he finished by leaving the button-hook in the boot. She pulled on an astrakhan bolero, and passed over her shoulder a strap from which hung a pair of racing glasses in a case. With her foot forward, standing in a fine pose, she stayed admiring herself, continually grimacing. George caught a glimpse of her reflection, and his eyes went wild, his nostrils dilated, and the blood rushed to his head. She ogled him from the corner of her eye, and turning round, said : "Let us go!"

He was at her feet, pressing his head against her petticoats; and embracing her thighs with his arms, he sobbed : "Wicked, wicked one!"

She bent over him, and placing her hand on his trousers, caressed his prick sweetly. "What? you think of nothing but fucking — we haven't got time. And then, you don't deserve that I should let you have me."

"Mercy!" he supplicated with joined hands. She pinched his ear, which she was pulling, and made him walk on his knees to the easy-chair, unbutton himself, and pull out his prick. She raised her dress to her knees and ordered him to hold it there. And she frigged him under the sole of her boot, whilst she was putting on her gloves; dominating him by her erect stature and penetrating him with her majesty.

94

The Mistress and the Slave

When she had frigged him under her delicate slipper, whilst exposing her pretty naked body, he had been subjugated by her lascivious grace. But now, in this bold costume, so becoming to her fiery beauty, with this tranquil manner of decking herself out, whilst the enslaved male palpitated beneath her, she seemed to him greater, more imposing and more haughty. Her very foot, in its tight boot, was more imperious and dominating.

When he found himself at her side in the carriage which took them to Auteuil, a flood of passion mounted to his lips. He was forced to cry out "Anna! Anna!"

She looked out of the window indifferently.

"Darling mistress! If you knew—Oh, yes, if you knew how I suffer, you would have pity—you are so pretty—so pretty! so beautiful! Nothing in the world is as beautiful and as pretty as you are. And no one can feel your beauty as I can. Anna, I beg you—your eyes—turn your beautiful eyes towards your slave."

"Don't excite yourself. You are going to make a pig of yourself. Listen. If you win at the races, you shall sleep with me, and I promise you a delicious night."

He laughed a loud laugh, hysterical and full of sobs, and began clucking, "I shall win! I shall win!"

She babbled pleasantly, and made him chat with her. His conversation was witty, and he looked at her, full

95

of astonishment. Who was this woman who could, when she wished, make him joyous or sad; make him pass, at her pleasure, from an inordinate infatuation to a peaceful quietude?

They went into the paddock as the first race was being run. George met a trainer whom he knew, and without leaving Anna, he questioned him.

"You know English then?"—"Very well. German also, and Russian, Spanish and Italian."—"I wish you would teach me English."—"Certainly. And when the pupil does not know her lesson she will punish the teacher."—"Dame! It is always the teacher's fault if the pupil does not learn."

They went to the booths where the betting took place, and following the trainer's tip George risked one hundred francs. The bell rang and the horses darted off. Every thing went well. Their horse, cleverly held in, had reached as far as the whip of the leading horse, when it fell at the water jump, and pitched its jockey off.

"It has lost!" said George. She looked sourly at him with tightened lips. All round were people gesticulating and joyous.

"They've won, haven't they? How much?"—"Wait. We don't know yet." The numbers were hoisted, and the price shown.

"How much would your five louis have brought in?"—"Six hundred francs. We should have touched seven hundred francs." — "We must win next race. Otherwise I shall leave you and go off with the Italian Marquis. Don't turn round. He is behind you devouring me with his eyes. He must have won, for he is flourishing banknotes."

George, upset, did not know what to do. He began to study the racing news. But everything was vague and contradictory. Feeling tired, he backed the newspaper tip; and it also lost. Anna made preparations for leaving him. She held out her hand loftily, with a cold look. However, he succeeded in drawing her on one side, near the railings, and begged her :

"Anna! My sainted Anna! Once more! A single time!"

"Very well! And thou wilt win—Win! I wish it!"

He trembled as with a physical shock, and a superstition sprang up in him. From the moment that she wished anything, it ought to happen. Was she not the All-Powerful itself? Still he remained undecided. What was he to back? Then his wandering look ran against the number-board. A hand appeared and put up number 11. He immediately remembered that he had first met her on the 11th November. He looked at the card and saw that the name of the horse was *Hard Love*. He no longer hesitated, but staked five hundred francs. With closed eyes, not wishing to see the race, he mentally repeated the name of the horse. People cried out;

and then there was a great silence. He opened his eyes and saw them putting up on the board number 11.

" Won ! " he said, without a muscle of his face moving. They hoisted the starting-price board. *Hard Love* was an outsider.

" How much ? "

" Eleven thousand five hundred francs. We receive twelve thousand francs." She stamped her feet, with a guttural and raucous laugh : the yelping of a hyena.

" Let us go ! " he murmured.

" No, I wish you to win more ; and we will have each other five times ! "

He had the winning number. Doubtless it was number 5. However, when he read the horse's name, he hesitated. *Requiem*. What a mournful name for a night of love !

He backed it, punting five hundred francs, and again won.

" Let us get off ! " she cried, joyously.

The light was waning. Their vehicle went along at a rapid pace.

" How much altogether ? " — " Nineteen thousand francs."—" I must see them ! Give them to me."

He took the banknotes by bundles, the louis by handfuls, and threw them in her lap.

" Thou hast no more ? This is all ? " — " All ! "—" Beware, if you 're lying ! "

He had to get up, and bend forward in front of her,
whilst she went through his pockets. In the left pocket
of his trousers, through the cloth, her hand met with
his stiff prick. She squeezed it with a quick and vigorous caress.

" Anna ! " he sighed.

" Lower the blinds ! "

And throwing the plunder into the reticule, she got
astride of George. Her belly did not flutter with large
undulations, but she had a sombre movement of her
arse, an abrupt and jerky shaking of her buttocks. He
spent, with his nose between her titties, breathing in
the strong odour, the lustful perfume which her skin
exhaled.

She was charming all the evening. After the theatre,
when they returned to her bed-room, the fête began.
George had his delicious night ! Kisses rained on his
face. He feverishly held forward his lips, but she
avoided them, kissing him on the eyes, on the cheeks,
in the neck. At last, with her two hands, she took his
head, threw it backwards, and lips against lips, with
mingled tongues, it was a long unspeakable kiss, which
ran through his marrow like a stream of love. And her
perfidious caresses ! Commencing by slight touches, light
as the brushing of a wing, and finishing by a brutal
suction, a nail-scratch, or a sharp pinching. She undressed. George took off her boots and stockings, de-

votedly kissing her white and chubby feet, his tongue
lingering under the sole, and wandering between the
toes. At last, he held her beneath him. But he had
passed through too many emotions. His too ardent
desire had finished by breaking him down, aud now his
nerves were foundered. As he straggled across Anna,
he perceived that he was becoming limp, and stopped,
feeling foolish. She began to laugh, but not mockingly.

"Don't be upset, little one. It's nothing." All the
same he was grieved. So near to happiness !

"Come on ! When I tell thee it's nothing ! You
know well, when thy Nana wishes it, there is nothing
more to say, it must come !"

Terrified, he said, " I beg you—not your hand !"

She screamed with laughter. " Are you frightened
then ?"

"You know it well ! It is by your hand that you
dominate me. And whether it is gentle or brutal, the
result is the same. It breaks me and infatuates me,
exasperates my desire. Certainly, don't do it ! When
you frig me, it does not satisfy me."

She listened to him, with a serious air, and said,
gravely : "Yes, I know. But I will not frig thee to-
night."

She opened the drawer of her night table, and took
out a riband, as wide as a finger. She wrapped it round
his balls, tightening it until the skin of the scrotum was

stretched. Then her hand grazed them, and George groaned with pleasure. Little by little his member swelled. Violet-tinted, it stood up, superb. Without leaving the ends of the riband, she drew George on her, and in to her cunt. And her powerful arse moved, with short quick jerkings, the quivering movements continuing, without intermission, until the spasm overtook him. Occasionally her hand tugged lightly at the riband.

He spent.

And he had the pleasure of seeing her spend also. Her features were drawn rigid, her eyes were hollow and sunken, and gradually a pallor, a grey shade, crossed her face. Beyond that, no movement, no cry. She washed herself.

George looked at her, with eyes filled with gratitude and love. She handed him the serviette wet with his prick, and devoted herself to a learned massage, with fingers more agile than spider-touches. She threw the serviette, and then rejoined him, and her hand wandered everywhere. She had a way of frigging the tips of his nipples which made him cry out. He writhed, and tried to tear himself away, but the clinging fingers followed his every movement.

He had another erection, and during a kiss, he wished to take her. She leapt to the bottom of the bed, and supporting herself by her two hands, she insisted on him placing himself behind her. But the treat which she presented to him was too beautiful. He knelt down, and licked and sucked with devotion. And she made him make love *en levrette*.[1] The friskings of her arse dragged passionate exclamations from him.

He slept with a heavy sleep, a dreamless sleep, when a keen sensation awoke him with a start. By the light of the night-lamp he saw her bending over him. She had thrown aside the coverings, and was forcibly sucking him.

"Oh! Darling mistress! No! I don't wish it! You are too beautiful—not that, I beg of you! It is I, who should—"

He could not finish. Without listening to him she continued her powerful suction, as irresistible as the clinging of a cupping glass. He spent, writhing. And the greedy mouth madly sucked him, until he was absolutely prostrated.

Ten o'clock was striking when he woke up. She was still sleeping. Her sweet face looked like a child's. He gazed at her devoutly, admiring her firm and white arms, her delicate profile, with its cheeky little nose, slightly turned up. When she stretched herself: "Thou hast slept well?"—"Yes, darling mistress!"

She immediately approached him and entwined her

[1] In the grey-hound fashion, *i.e.* the woman bends down, and the man has her from behind.

supple and warm body around him. He felt her every-where about him, as though tied with a climber.

"And you want to make love?"

He did not reply, his head was buried in her arm-pit, the intoxicating perfume of which he was drinking. She ran her fingers along his body, drawing quiverings from it. And brusquely she flung herself upon him, dominating him with her slender bust. She was a powerful rider, giving him blows of the loins which crushed him.

He begged: "A kiss! A kiss!"

She bent down. Mouth against mouth, with mingled tongues, they swooned.

At breakfast, she re-counted their winnings.

"There's too much for the savings bank."

"Certainly!" said George, smiling. "A bank preferably."

"Good! You shall take me with you. It will be the beginning of my fortune. At seventeen years old, nineteen thousand francs, that's not bad, I think. And, as you pass your office, you'll take a thousand francs, and that will make a round sum."

During an entire week George knew every delight, every human refinement of love, naive and perverse caresses. But it always finished with copulation, the natural drawing together of the sexes.

But one evening when he arrived, joyous, he shuddered at finding her with her serious air, a cold look.

"Come!"

He followed her, trembling. When they were in the bed-room, she planted herself in front of him.

"Why hast thou lied to me?"

He stammered: "In what? I swear to you—"

He did not finish. A rain of blows stunned him.

"Undress thyself!"

She brought out the whip.

"Kiss it!"

He wished to speak, to clear himself, but she imposed silence on him. On his knees, with joined hands, he had to kiss the whip. Capriciously, she threw it in its corner, bent down George's neck, and sitting on his back, she took off one of her slippers, and gave him a thrashing with it, then she sat in the easy-chair.

"Come here, so that I can frig thee!"

He stammered: "What have I done then?"

Already her hand was on him. She took the bridle, a pinch of flesh, between her first finger and the thumb, and shook it rapidly. George felt a new sensation which terrified him. He was still spending when she slung her foot in his arse.

"You told me the races were over! They are on next week at Nice. We are going there."

At Nice, intuition was rebellious. In spite of the most subtle deductions, George could not touch a winner.

"I know why," said Anna.

That evening in the hotel, he had to lie on the carpet, stretched all his length, perfectly naked.

"I am going to shit in thy mouth.   There is nothing more than my beautiful shit needed to bring luck."

He implored her not to, but she kept him restrained under her look.   He had to submit to the humiliation. She even opened his mouth and rubbed it in his teeth.

The next day he backed *Doux Espoir,* a gain of three thousand francs, which the roulette table at Monte Carlo again added to.

"How much?" Anna asked.

"Sixteen thousand francs altogether!"

"Good!   Pack your bag, and we will go back to Paris."

George longed to be there.   When he had Anna at his side he scarcely ever thought of his wife.

When he got home he met the doctor, who, as he went out, reproved him sharply.   "It is curious that you neglect a young charming wife, one of the prettiest women in Paris!   Doubtless, for some whore!"

George made a sign of protestation.

"Listen!   If I speak to you thus, it is because I have the right to do so.   Your wife is condemned. How much time has she to live?   That depends on you.   If you continue in your present manner, you will bury her in less than a year."

He went out, leaving George speechless.

But he finished by shaking his head, as though he wished to shake away the unpleasant thought—these medical men, if one were forced to believe them! And he was delighted with his wife's colour. The hectic roses of consumption bloomed on her cheeks. She had a superb carnation tint, and her beautiful eyes shone with the brightness of stars. Her imploring look invited George to sweet caresses. He felt a revolt, an aversion of the flesh. What good trying? He could never be unfaithful to Anna.

"It would do you no good. Get better first."

Blushing with an adorable vivacity she hid her head against her husband's breast.

"Alas!" she said, ingenuously, "what your neglect makes me do is far worse."—"What then?"—"In the night I imagine I have you in my arms and I caress myself."—"Foolish little one!" and he went to rejoin his Anna.

His passion turned into a monomania, his whole mental state became entirely transferred to his mistress. Everything he did or thought he reported to her; often in a most extraordinary manner. In the middle of a serious conversation the person to whom he was speaking would with astonishment see him pull a piece of money out of his pocket, look at it, and then put it back where he had taken it from; his face shining or darkened. He wished to see if Anna was going to welcome his visit or not; if she would consent to make love; if at least she would kiss him. If the coin came out head the augury was propitious; if tail it was uulucky. Although the result showed how unreliable these forecasts were, George would begin again next day. In the street, at home, in company, he pulled out his coins from his pocket, and consulted them aside.

He rarely dined at home. He got to the Avenue Mac-Mahon about six o'clock. If she had not come in, he waited for her feverishly. They commenced the English lessons; and she learnt quickly and well. Then they dined, either at her place, or at a restaurant.

But for the last fortnight, she would no longer give herself to him. He had slept with her, and she refused him. He had begged and wept, and she imposed silence on him, and had peacefully gone to sleep. By the light of the night-lamp, he devoured her with his eyes for hours, for insomnia made his martyrdom draw out. But he avoided even a sigh, fearing to trouble her rest. In the morning when she woke up he again implored her. They were both dressed. He was going away, gloomy and resigned, when with a push she threw him backwards on the bed, and rapidly unbuttoned him. And she frigged him in a manner which in one minute brought to life again the terror of the night.

The next day she sent him away immediately after

dinner, wishing him to attend to his election work. Then she consented to his taking her to the Latin quarter, where she went every evening now. Or, perhaps, she passed all her nights there! The cab stopped at the angle of the rue Cujas and the boulevard St-Michel. George had to wait there for her return. Anna got out, and went he knew not where. Immediately the cab started his torture began. She squared herself on the seat, pressing him against the side of the cab. And the warmth of her body, penetrating the cloth, kindled a fever in George. He grew drunk with hearing her speak, and his nostrils dilated with the effuvium of her fatal odour. He succeeded in dissimulating his discomfort, but she gave him light and perfidious touchings. She would drop something on George's knee, and in picking it up her fingers came against his prick, as if by accident. Carried away, he would implore her; and then she seized it, and frigged it. When the cab was not far on its way, she went gently, with a slow caress, always increasing in force and speed, and nerve-shattering. But sometimes they were already at Cluny, when he commenced his solicitations. Then it was a rapid and brutal massage. She seemed to materialise her will. He felt her annihilating his own, and substituting hers. However fatigued he might be, when Anna's hand held him, he was forced to spend. Immediately she uttered, " I wish it ! " the sperm sprang out.

Sometimes she ignored George's emotion, and continued chattering. He would take her hand, and place it on his prick. Her wicked smile came, and she did not resist, but let her hand go where he wished. Already he was quivering at her contact, when he thought of the effort, the pain in his nerves and muscles, the labour and the falseness of the artifice. The thought of the sufferings afterwards, terrified him still more. How he knew them! Gloomy prostration, stupidity, longing. Ah! this longing without power, so keen! This longing always more acute, in the keen biting of the flesh. All the desperate and vain ardour which took possession of him when she had frigged him. He thrust her hand away. She let it go, continuing to smile, and he writhed under the anguish which was always increasing. Whirlwinds of flame ran through his veins, struck at his brain, burnt into his glazed eyes. Panting, he would implore her, in a nervous voice. And suddenly she would seize him, and working it roughly: "Spend! I wish it!"—"Yes! yes! Oh, Anna! Anna darling!"

And he would spend, groaning. Then a nervous cough shook him, and he would remain prostrate. He lamented over himself. Why did she refuse herself? Was he not her faithful and devoted slave? Did she want more money?

She shrugged her shoulders :

" If I wanted thy money, I should go to thy house. and would take everything, even thy wife's bed."

When she spoke thus, he trembled, full of a terror which turned to desire. He felt that she spoke the truth. Besides, he no longer even tried to struggle. What good was it?

One evening, when he came to dinner, she introduced a guest to him.

" Doctor Ernest."

He was a tall and lanky blonde of twenty-five years of age, with a good-looking insipid face. The rest of him was insignificant. They were a little stiff at first. but Anna, very correct, treated the two men with equal politeness, and spared George her usual " thou" in the presence of the stranger.

But as eleven o'clock struck, and neither of them spoke of going, she got impatient.

" Thou canst be off. To-morrow! As usual!"

George turned pale, and, raising his head, he said to the other man,

" We can go along together. What do you say ?"

Ernest, ill at ease, got up awkwardly, when Anna. putting her hand on his arm, commanded,

" Thou art going to sit down again."

And threatening George with her wicked expression, " Come !"

He followed her, encouraging himself to revolt. This

time, it need not be said, cost what it might, he must break the chain.   Everything has its limit!

As she entered the bed-room, she threw off her dressing gown and chemise, and in black silk stockings and red satin slippers, she took her stand in front of the mirror, having seemingly quite forgotten George.   She threw back her torso, took her breasts in her two hands, made them spring forward, and balancing herself on her haunches, moved her buttocks sideways, uncovered her teeth, closed her eyes, and then dilated them widely. It was a strange mimicry, mysterious as a rite.   He approached her slowly, fascinated; and weeping, he kissed her on the nape of the neck.   She pushed her neck back, tickling his face with its down.   And with long aspirations, he breathed in her perfume.   She disengaged herself, and slowly turning, showed him her entire figure.

"It's true I'm not too badly shaped.   Look at me well, my dear.   Look, for I have an idea that you will not see me much oftener."

He knelt before her, licking her slippers, and sobbing wildly, whilst tears ran down his cheeks.   She quietly sat down in the easy-chair.

"Here! so that I can frig thee."

"No! No! Anna—dear mistress, not now.   I am so unhappy—"

"Come!"

He came close to her, and knelt at her feet.

"No! Stand up! As at Ménilmontant. You shall spend standing up—right on your trotters. You will be more fatigued, more worn out."

She took him. Her extended fingers touched nothing, but the extremity of the gland was imprisoned in the palm of her hand, and she pressed strongly on the lips of the meatus. The prick wheeled round, shaking madly.

"Ah! Ah! Mistress! Oh, how you make me suffer!"

"Spend, you filthy beast!"

He reeled forward, almost falling, and clung to the arms of the easy-chair. She thrust him back, and he had to spend standing up, with the spasm made keener by her cruel hand.

He fell down. With a blow of her foot she made him stand up again.

"Undress thyself!"

He stood naked before her, awaiting her orders.

"On thy knees!"

She pressed his head down until his forehead touched the carpet. With a foot on his neck, she made her whip whistle through the air, and cried: "Ernest! Here!"

George implored her, sobbing: "Mercy! Dearest mistress! Mercy—oh, not that! No! No!"

She repeated: "Ernest! Wilt thou come? Must I go and fetch thee?"

Ernest came in, awkward and embarrassed, and ran and crouched in the shadow. Anna lashed George' buttocks, flogging for a considerable time, whilst he re mained gloomy and impassible, and closed his eyes. Bu he re-opened them when, with the end of her whip, she tickled his behind. With little blows of the lash she sought out his balls, and in the glass George saw the group. Standing haughtily, she resembled a gladiatoi treading with disdainful foot on the neck of the van quished. She drew back: "Stay where you are!"

Throwing aside the whip, she bent down, and fingered his nipples, rubbed his prick, and triturated his balls. He had a cockstand. "Lie down, flat on your stomach."

She did not leave hold of his prick, which she pulled backwards. She pressed the tip of her foot on the bridle of his member, and frigged him by the shaking of her nervous leg, under the hard sole of her satin slipper.

He spent again. All his will-power had left him, and he felt so miserable and humiliated—shrivelled up and humbler than ever under the terror of his inexorable mistress.

"Then you find me not sufficiently beautiful to pay me more than a slave? Yes! If during the last fortnight I have not given myself to thee, it is because I had a fancy for Ernest. And what would you say if I let myself be fucked by him here, in front of you?"

He looked at her with submissive eyes, the eyes of a

poor beaten dog which still trembles, begging the caress of pardon.

" Go on your knees, on this chair. Bend down, with your hands on the ground. There—you are going to hold the candle. This won't be dull."

She took a candle, scraped its sides, and trimmed the edges. Lighting it, she stuck it into George's behind.

" Beware of moving !"

She stepped back to judge of the effect, like an artist enamoured of his work.

" That's perfect! But it wants a something. A favour, a knot of riband."

She chose a riband and looked round her.

" Shit! I can't find my pin-cushion. At any rate, you can replace it."

She took some needles from a case, and pushed them into George's buttocks, on the two sides of the candle. Then she called : " Ernest, here !"

George felt a melancholy trembling, his heart tightened with shame and disgrace. But he did not move. Ernest also recoiled. But, the same as George, he submitted to Anna's ascendancy. She repeated : " Come !"

He came. " Undress thyself !"

In a minute he was naked, with a grotesque thinness. " Suck me off !"

She threw herself back on the edge of the bed. On his knees on the carpet, Ernest sucked. Suddenly she seized him, and threw him in her place which she quitted, on his back at the edge of the bed.   Going to George, she wrapped the riband round his balls, and tightening it, encircled his entire prick with numerous turnings, and tied it round the bridle.   Holding the ends in her hand, she went to Ernest, and got on him, riding him with continuous jerkings of her powerful bottom, whilst she gave the cord a terrible shaking.   The two men spent at the same time, blending in the same cry their passion for their victor.

She sent them away.   " To-morrow, at midnight.   The first who comes will wait in the street for the other."

They went out, horribly embarrassed.   When they shook hands outside, there was, in their clasp, quite a fellowship of passion and suffering, the tacit acceptance of the inevitable.

Next day, Anna inverted the roles.   She thrust George backwards on the edge of the bed, and rode him, turning her back to him.   The frisking of her spirited crupper compelled him to spend, whilst, in front of her, Ernest corkscrewed his meagre body under her hand, groaning lamentably.

VII

In this great Paris where the moving crowd hears
and repeats the oracles of the gutter press, by that
means alone Anna's celebrity grew and increased. Her
carnal beauty, haloed by luxury, had made a sensation.

She had been noticed at the theatre, at the races.
They had seen her at Monte-Carlo, at Nice. Always
correct, and impeccable in her manner. The most
malicious had been put at fault, and avowed that they
knew not how to class her. Her entire person seemed
an enigma. Whence did she come? Was she merely
a Parisienne? Some quoted the effrontery of her beauty,
her sovereign grace, her sure taste, her manner of wearing her toilettes; others represented that it is from the
provinces, and from abroad, that the most accomplished
types of Parisiennes are recruited.

Young and old, all the men about town who watch
for fresh women, had attempted to approach her. They
had all had an attempt at her, and when the way was
open to them, they found themselves astounded at their
conquest. For, from the beginning, she held such an

empire that they dared not infringe the secret imposed upon them. She tossed them off, tamed them, and made them pay dearly. Women were equally struck with her.

An Austrian princess sent her a pearl necklace in a bouquet of orchids ; and, cooling her heels in her ante-chamber, she begged that Madame would receive her.

Introduced, the princess, tall and stately, stood upright in front of Anna, who, impertinent and affected, and stretched in an easy-chair, continued to take stock of her.

"So thou art the princess? One would rather have said a servant!"

She got up, and ducked her head for a bow.

"Look at me: I am of the people. Dost thou believe that I have more distinction than thou hast?"

"Yes, madame."

"Call me Majesty."

"Yes, Majesty."

She sat down again, and insisted on the princess kneeling, and taking off her shoes. Continuing to treat her as a servant, she made her undress her. When she was naked, she ordered the princess to undress herself also. And when, trembling with emotion and desire, the foreign lady got embarrassed with her corset laces, she inflicted on her arms and buttocks a volley of blows from her whip, under which the other writhed, cringed, and licked her feet.

However, she succeeded in undressing herself.

Anna threw her back on the couch, frigged her nipples till the breasts fell exhausted, and pulled the hair from her cunt. The princess, crying and sobbing, begged a kiss.

But Anna, thrusting her forward, put her on all fours, at the spot which she had just made her leave.

"You are going to suck my cunt, and put your tongue up my arse—show how you can work."

The Austrian darted her tongue. Pulling open with her two hands the robust buttocks, she made it penetrate stiff and pointed into the dainty hole, and caused it to vibrate there. Already Anna was sighing. Substituting a finger, she withdrew her tongue, which she slowly ran along the furrow as far as the vulva. She pushed into the vagina, whose walls she struck with rapid movements. Then she mounted to the clitoris, which she tickled with the lapping of her tongue, and suddenly, without the agile tongue stopping its frisking, the princess took it between her lips and ardently sucked it.

Anna writhed under the enjoyment of this amorous mouth.

Then the Austrian nibbled the clitoris, and struck it with the tip of her tongue. Anna spent. A flood of spunk sprang from her womb, and drenched the lips of the gougnotte.[1]

[1] *Gougnotte*, a woman who sucks another woman's vagina.

"Is your Majesty content?" the princess timidly asked.

Without deigning to reply, Anna raised herself, and laid her on the easy-chair. Her hands wandered all over the Austrian's body, drawing quivers from it. Distractedly, with her voice full of sobs, the princess implored a kiss. Anna gave her one. And as the foreigner was gluttonously sucking her tongue, she put a knee on her neck, and, with her nail, frigged her till the blood came.

For a whole week the Austrian groaned whenever with her scarified backside she touched a chair, but she wrote to her intendant, in her own country, to sell the most important of her estates; and she established herself definitely in Paris. At the Avenue Kleber, in the mansion which the princess had acquired, Anna deigned occasionally to show herself on reception days. And she went to the fêtes, taking a noticeable place amongst the proudest aristocrats.

Her humour towards George remained fantastic, and full of caprices which nothing could explain. She called him, sent him away, and kept him without any possible reason. He could never foretell how he would be received. Without apparent motive, she was sweet even to wheedling, or she frigged him to death, bullied him, and ill-treated him. Or, worse still, she treated him pleasantly, with an infernal coquetry, until, distracted, he desired and begged for the snare of her hand, the false and depressing caress.

But she never tolerated his having her. He did not even try any longer, knowing that it always finished badly. And, always with a new anguish, he awaited her good pleasure. So it was she who had him, varying the attitudes. In addition to those which she had already taken with him, she invented others, simple and complex. She made him kneel in front of her, crouching under him, or kneeling herself. Then, placing him in her vagina, she brought on the discharge by her wrigglings. Another time it was on the bed : on their knees, face to face. When she had put him in her, she let herself go gently backwards, and George had to do the same thing, so that the feet of each of them framed the other's head. By a gentle quivering she brought on the ejaculation. At other times, George had to lie along two chairs, his loins between them, whilst she vigorously rode his immovable and stiff body. In bed, with their heads on each other's parts, she stretched herself along him, as he lay on his back, and pushed it in her cunt. He saw her thus foreshortened, with delicate calves and superb croup. She would stoop over his feet which she tickled, and with balancing herself, would produce a keen spasm. At times, they remained a long time chatting, without her permitting a word of love; whilst she made him assist at her most intimate toilette. His desire, increasing little by little, would reach to frenzy. He went on talking about any trivial thing, but he stammered, and his eyes showed a love petition. Yet, already he was fearing the fatal caress. She pretended to know nothing, redoubled her coquetries, and placed herself in her most seductive attitudes. She infatuated him with her smiles, and burnt him with her sombre look. Already she was dressed, to go out. Sighing, he would take his hat, to follow her, when, at the door, she would push him against the wall, unbutton him with a turn of her hand, and raising her skirts, would encunt him. With a few movements of her croup, she brought on the spasm, a violent spasm which left George stupid, with limp legs. When she had given herself to him, several times after some hours of tenderness, he lay stretched on the bed at her side, his limbs weakened and languid. He looked at her with devotion. She would smile, and taking him with her hand:

"Darling mistress, have pity. It was so sweet and calming. And I cannot do it again."

"You must! I wish it!"

He stiffened his neck and thighs, and groaned, with his entire being strained towards his release. But fatigue pressed on him, and his members relaxed. However the magician hand insisted. She dragged his nerves to lust. So he stiffened his muscles, and gave to this sterile ejaculation the sad imitation of love. One evening it was nine o'clock, and she had not wanted to go out. Clad in a diaphanous wrapper, her naked feet in soft slippers, she was lying along the easy-chair, with George kneeling in front of her.

" So, you are now on the municipal council of Paris. That is something; above all, if you know how to manoeuvre. Besides you will do nothing without first consulting me. I want to remove, and I have seen a flat in the Avenue du Bois which pleases me. The rent is twenty thousand francs. You will go to-morrow and take it in my name."

" And the furniture? What there is here will not be sufficient."

" Don't bother yourself. I will do everything that is needful."

" It is true. You are rich."

She threw on him an undefinable look. He understood, and hung his head down. But since the scene at Ménilmontant, and, above all, the night when he had been whipped in front of Ernest, he no longer dare show her that he knew anything.

She got up, threw off her wrapper, and appeared radious in her splendid nudity. " Undress thyself !"

She sat down, and drew him to her. With his feet and hands touching the ground, he had to lie with his stomach over her knees. She took his prick between her thighs, and tightened on it more and more with a slow compression, whilst her hand gently tickled his behind.   He spent: a fervent beatitude, full of ecstasy.

"Swine! Your spunk's running down my legs. Wipe them.   There!   Come and sit down.   It ought not to cost you much to procure a journalist's card."—" For you?"—" No, imbecile! For you!"—" It is easy. But what for?"—"You will learn that to-morrow."

Whilst speaking, she was running her hand all over him, and a wave of quiverings was already spreading over George's body.   His prick stood.   She chose a riband, passed it round his balls, and tightened it until the scrotum was stretched.   Without leaving the riband, she rubbed him with the other hand, with a rapid, energetic friction.   He spent, writhing.

"You have tact, you talk well, and have a good appearance.   And with the languages you know—"

"What then?"

"When does the Exhibition open?"

"Three weeks hence."

"Good!   There is no time to lose.   My little one, you must get the journalist's card at once.   You will go round to the principal hotels in Paris.   You will speak to the manager and show him your card and tell him you wish to act as guide to distinguished foreigners, to initiate them into the pleasures of the capital."

George listened to her stupified.   In spite of everything he was forced to interrupt her.

"But it's absurd!"

"What do you say?"

With a thrust she placed him upright, and got up. Putting an arm round his waist, she bent him over her knee, and fixing his head under her armpit, she intoxicated him with her perfume. Already he had an erection. She lodged the gland in her palm, and with her flat extended hand, she turned rapidly. The prick, madly shaken, also turned. George groaned:

"Wicked, wicked woman! Pity! I will obey."

The arm which was round him slipped lower, and she poked a finger into his bottom.

"Spend!"

He discharged, with groans.

She knocked him into the easy-chair with a heavy blow.

"When you've seen the manager, you will arrange with the hotel porter. You will repeat your story, and slip a louis into his hand, and promise him a share of your profits!"

"But your design? I don't see it."

"You will know by-and-bye."

She went to the toilette table, and covered her hands with a lather of soap. Going to George, she took him by the prick, and pulled him to the edge of the couch. There she frigged him vigorously, and her left forefinger, slipping into his behind, penetrated to the prostate, tormenting him incessantly.   He discharged.

"Anna! Anna!   Enough!   You are killing me!"

"What do I care!   For a long time I have wanted to frig thee till the blood comes."

Terrified, he grovelled in front of her, licking her feet, and stammering fragments of phrases, and incoherent nothings.

"You bore me!   Pass me the newspaper.   Lie on the floor; on your back.   You'll serve as a footstool."

She settled herself in the easy-chair, and read, with crossed legs, and one foot on George's stomach.   He did not move.   Half an hour passed.   She crushed the paper into a ball, threw it away, and with a shake, sent her slippers flying across the room, and took his prick between her naked feet.   The top of his cock rested against the instep of one foot, whilst she rubbed the bridle with the sole of the other, and her nail scratched his balls.   This lasted a long time, but eventually he discharged, so prostrated that he scarcely stirred.   She put on her stockings and shoes, which he had to button ; and then he had to stop on his knees in front of her, seated in the easy chair.   Each time that fatigue made his thighs bend, with a thrust of her muscular leg she sent her toe straight between his buttocks, putting him upright on his knee-caps.   A half hour passed by.   She took his prick with her whole hand, encircling the bridle, and frigged it roughly.   He was compelled to spend.

The sperm came out mingled with blood.   He was still discharging when she said :

" Then it's understood ?   Thy business in the hotels ? Of course you won't deal with any but the best people. And if the chap is worth the trouble, if he has plenty of money, you will bring him to me."

" Anna ! "

" What !   Do you want me to start again ?   You have no more spunk in your balls, but there is blood ! and I will undertake to make it spurt out.   And if there needs anything further to decide thee, I tell thee, I will shit in thy throat."

He bent his head in agreement.   With her cruel smile playing over her face, she gave him her hand to kiss, and sent him away.

A fortnight later, in the flat in the Avenue du Bois, the furnishers were striking the last blows of the hammer. The Austrian princess had chosen the gallery's most beautiful pictures.   A Watteau and a Fragonard formed a contrast with gloomy Spanish canvases.   And Flemish masters seemed melancholy at the side of a flamboyant Titian.

A Hungarian noble, an octogenarian who had not had an erection for the last fifteen years, had fallen under her gloomy glance.   Every week Anna gave him an afternoon.   She excited him so well that he showed himself at his best.   She rubbed his prick against her clitoris, and half fucked, half frigged, she forced the old man to spend.

He sent to her the most precious things he had in his château at Bude, the old Turkish town. Heavy and bizarre jewelry, and cabinets encrusted with mother-of pearl, were sent to Paris by express train.

A Belgian gave the dining-room furniture. Cordovan leathers, and oak furniture which had been carved like lace.

The Marquis of Cazzavoglio returned from Florence with an entire room, torn from a palace of the Medicis. Monstrances veneered with tortoiseshell and silver, embellished with miniatures; Turkish marbles.

And with death in his soul, George went in quest of foreigners, pigeons to be plucked by his mistress. In an hotel near the Alma the porter presented him to a Russian boyard.

"You are a journalist?"

"Yes, sir, here is my card."

"Very good! Then you can show me some curious things. You see I speak French—like a Russian. And your conditions—?"

"Whatever you wish."

"That's not foolish. You please me."

George looked at him. He had never seen a man so hairy. Hair up to his eyes; and a colossus. He was almost six feet six inches in height and was broad in proportion, with the build of an athlete.

"You must love women!"

"That shows itself, doesn't it? But I mistrust your Parisian women! There was one who cost me a hundred thousand roubles. For a squealing singer that was rather dear!"

"You were generous!"

"Not at all! But, all the same, you can't guess—when I was only a child, my joy was to torment little girls. With the peasants, and the moujiks' daughters, that didn't matter. But one day, my aunt from Petersburg came to the château with her daughter, a girl twelve years old. I was ten. 'Nadia,' said my aunt, 'go into the garden and play with your cousin Dmitri.' The little one, who had the manners of a lady, took my arm. We went into the garden, which is as big as a park. She offered me her packet of sugar-plums. I snatched it from her hand, and began to stuff myself with the bonbons. She laughed, and said to me, 'You are not polite, or you would offer me some.' I looked at her. A droll idea came to me. I seized the little one, sat down on a seat, I pulled her clothes up, and threw her across my knees, with her legs in the air, and one after another, I thrust the bonbons into her bottom and in her vulva—Ha! ha! ha! If you had heard her cry, you would laugh as I do. But afterwards it was another story! I felt the knout. Eh! we are wandering from the singer, the Parisian girl. It was at Kiew. I had invited her to supper, and had drunk too much, and had a heavy hand. I do not know why, but I struck at her. She drew back her head, and the ends of my fingers broke her nose, disfiguring her permanently. I was afraid of being sent to the mines. You see they would have certainly sent me to Siberia, because she was a Frenchwoman. I preferred to pay a hundred thousand roubles. But all the same, it turned me against your compatriots. Still, one can see! Only, tell me, what pleasure can you find with a woman who has not been warmed? Talk to me about a pretty girl who has just been flogged! Do you know that flagellation is quite an art? You must slap fast and hard without cracking the skin, or letting a drop of blood spurt out. In my country most people fasten the woman on a seat with straps. No need of all this apparatus. I easily hold a woman's two wrists in my left paw. I lay down the lady, no matter where, on her stomach. I have a good whip. A handle easy to hold, three long strips of supple leather. To start with, a blow across the shoulders. The thongs must separate, so that the ends reach the two armpits. The little one cries out already—by-and-bye, she will know better why. Without hurrying, you go down to the fall of the loins. There must be streaks everywhere, all the back must be red. You then make a pause, long enough to smoke a cigarette—and then

129

you pass to the legs, one after the other. A sharp blow on each calf, then in the bend of the knee, up to the beginning of the arse, taking care to strike on the inside of the thighs, where the skin is tenderer. Then the whore writhes! Convulsions! You must hear her howl! But this is nothing yet. The real game commences when the thongs bite her buttocks. Then you slap quick and hard—another cigarette! But you must throw it away after the third whiff—then at random and vigorously you hit between the thighs, so that the three thongs coming together strike the vagina and the hair, sinking into the hollow of the buttocks, crushing the perineum, and bruising the edges of the vulva. You repeat the blow five or six times. And, to finish, if you are skilful, the middle thong strikes full on the clitoris, whilst the others lash the folds of the groin. It is a noticeable fact that if they cry, weep and groan, they love it, because instead of tightening their buttocks and closing their vulvas, they spread open everything, showing that they are on heat. My dear chap, try, you will tell me the result. A woman so cooked is tender and savoury. A chicken! She wheedles, she is hot, she spends ten times to your once. The whip makes the toughest arses tender. Ha! ha! ha! That is so!"

He laughed, and his laugh rolled with a bellowing sound; the laughter of a colossus, a good sort, who wants nothing but pleasure. George listened to him, stupefied; and hastened to leave him, and went to Anna's, whom he told what he had heard. She listened to him tranquilly.

"Very good! Here's a bear! You will bring him to me!"

"Darling mistress, you won't think of it."

She shrugged her shoulders, and making him cringe beneath her wicked look, repeated: "You will bring him."

That same evening George introduced the Russian, whom Anna, quite gracious. retained for dinner. He ate greedily and filthily. The sauce streamed down his beard. He scraped it off with his fingers, which he wiped on his serviette. However, he knew how to remain a great lord, with easy and simple manners. He looked persistently at Anna. She intoxicated him with her smiles, made him drunk by the amorous inflections of her voice, and penetrated him with the effluvia of her sombre looks. At dessert, she made a sign to George who, excusing himself, left them. The boyard, swinging his chair round, approached Anna. His eyes projected, shining with fever, and his face became conjested, but his voice remained calm.

"At last alone! But not enough so! Let us go to bed!"

She smiled maliciously, and put her hand underneath his nose.

"Fi, wicked one! Will you hold your tongue!"

Her hand was moist. The perfume of luxury com-
)leted the Russian's intoxication. His countenance
urned purple. He stammered :

"Not at all! I feel in good spirits."

Lifting Anna in his arms, in two steps he was in the
)ed-room. She did not struggle, but laughed.

"You are very strong. But in love you are a ninny."

And as, without replying to her, he placed her on the
)ed,

"You think perhaps that I am badly made. Let me
undress myself!"

She spoke in her slow voice with its metallic inflec-
ions :

"You are going to carry me to the easy-chair. And
you will come and sit at my side, I wish it!"

He obeyed. All his vast body trembled, shaken by
:he pangs of desire. Anna arranged herself, in a ravishing attitude, and throwing open her wrapper, she uncovered her legs. The man sighed, and breathed in
large gasps. At last she condescended to notice him.

"You are a savage! I will wager that you don't
even know what a kiss is."

She threw his head back, and penetrated him to the
marrow with the savour of her tongue. And without
leaving his lips, prolonging the enervating contact, she
unbuttoned him. She gently frigged him with a large

and slow movement, which went from the beginning of his balls to the extremity of his gland. He sighed heavily, full of anguish, filled with an unknown languor. He spent. And Anna's hand, more pressing and rapid, made the spasm keener.

She drew back, and looked down at him, triumphant. He stayed there prostrate and confused. Suddenly he burst out:

"Filthy bugger! You've tossed me off. You shall see."

Without moving from his place, he seized her by the wrist, and bent her arm with a slow and irresistible twist. Anna was doubled up and bent forward, and the pain drew a cry from her. He continued to hold her, pressing at the same time on her arm and back, bending her spine, and making her buttocks project. Without hurrying himself he lifted her skirts. In her slow, even voice, her authoritative voice, she said:

"Take care what you are doing. I shall make you pay dear. Already you belong to me more than you think."

He remained undecided, terrified at what was passing inside him. He left go of her. Adjusting himself, he pulled on his hat, and went off without turning his head. At once he ran to his hotel, upset everybody to get his bill and luggage, and was taken to the station, where he leapt into the first departing train. His destination

133

mattered little to him, provided that he got away from this woman who made him afraid. Next day, when Anna told him the story, George marvelled. He looked at her with admiration mingled with fright. What then was this strange charm which so brusquely inverted that which is most fixed in the human brain: the erotic conception? He thought of Catholic fiction, of succubi, of incarnate demons in the bodies of women who frigged and sucked ascetics to death; forcing to the work of the flesh the saints themselves, so frigid, debilitated, and almost unsexual by their macerations.

He acted as guide to an Englishman, a rosy and light-haired giant, twenty-two years old. He had not come to Paris to spree about with women. When George spoke of women, he explained frankly:

"No! I have my fiancée. I love her and am loved. We are both virgin, and it is through marriage that we shall learn pleasure."

"How nice that is!" Anna said. "This afternoon bring him at the Exhibition to the machine gallery."

She was there, clad simply, and modest in appearance. She was speedily at their side, stood in front of a dynamo. She fixed the lad with a persistent look, at once candid and impudent. Her parasol slipped from her fingers, and fell against the Englishman's legs. She stooped quickly and caught it, and her fingers skimmed his prick. The unlucky parasol, badly caught, wobbled, and again fell. In reaching for it, the perfidious hand renewed and prolonged the touching. Anna raised herself, blushing, stammered a few words of excuse in English, and was lost in the crowd. The young Englishman stood silent and overwhelmed, his thoughts wandering into the tumultuous disorder of his senses. At last he found his tongue.

"She is charming! How pretty she is! Where can one find her?"

George made a vague gesture of carelessness:

"Paris is full of them!"

"No!" said the other, with conviction. "I would give everything to see her again."

"Let us go then to the boulevard. One has the best chance there to find lost women."

They sat outside a café. Suddenly the Englishman cried out with joy, sprang up, jostling the passers-by, and joined Anna. She made a little difficulty at first, but finished by accepting a drink, and then a dinner and a theatre. And in the cab, with her light touches she let loose another storm in the novice's veins.

She took his virginity. Softened by the idyll, she spared him her sickly refinements, the mortal caress. And when she had stripped him of his last sovereign, she sent him home to his fiancée.

George brought others. Gross Americans, skinflint Germans, humpbacked Dutchmen, ostentatious Orientals, magnificent English, trooped through the flat in the Avenue du Bois.

With these people Anna went out, paraded herself, and pushed them into expense. The presence of George —guide and interpreter—safeguarded everything.

One day at the Exhibition, on the arm of a Spaniard, more laden with jewels than a shrine, she called George.

"I am stifling. Here! Carry my cape. And take my parasol and fan. Take the lot!"

On looking at him, she burst out laughing.

"But you look like a flunkey! In future I shall call thee Baptiste."

The outrage cut him to the heart. However, with a bitter smile, he murmured, "As Madame pleases!"

For several weeks she called him nothing else.

"Here Baptiste! Baptiste, go to the milliner, and tell her I want my hat at once."

And he had to put up with these insults with a smiling air, for if he showed his grief, she frigged him.

Following the old style, she returned to the slave all that he could give.

She gave him the post of her secretary of gallantries. To him fell the task of writing the replies to her adorers' letters. She furnished brief notes, which he had to embroider. Ironical or kind, she wished her letters to be full of spirits, sparkling with wit. If by chance, the writer was awkward, she made the whip whistle.

One evening, at the Trocadéro, she was alone with
George. Above the hum of the crowd, there was a
rolling sound of tambourines, a clanging of cymbals.
In front of a Moorish theatre, on the platform, a man
dressed in black was the performer, and a negress posed,
offering herself to the admiration of the loungers.

"Look!" cried Anna, clapping her hands. "It's me
in bronze."

In fact it was her Arab type, more accentuated. The
vulgar nose a little upturned, the large eyes, the mouth
with its strong lips, the round and muscular arms, the
swelling bust, and the tight and rebounding buttocks.

"I want her! Go—hurry up!"

George had to arrange first with the impresario, and
then with the negress. Anna scarcely consented to let
her finish her performance, and did not quit the booth
without taking away "the beautiful Aïscha."

VIII

I<small>N</small> the month of June, in the heavy sadness of a summer's day, George's wife passed away. At the foot of the bed between his two daughters, George yielded to an impulse. He hastened to write Anna a letter breaking things off. The next day, Anna came to his house. Trembling with anger, he ordered the importunate to be shown out. And, as he did so, he hesitated. His perplexity increased, and he quite lost his head.

He recalled his man, and told him twice over to show in the lady. He received her with an icy excess of politeness. She appeared very dignified, holding herself in, so as not to burst out laughing.

" How dare you write this letter? "

Avoiding looking at her, moved by her mere presence, he tried to harden his voice, striving to make her understand that he thought it best to part. Besides, he was determined. Whilst speaking, he rivetted his eyes on Anna's foot, with which she was nervously tapping the floor. He was horribly pale, and so oppressed that his voice hissed.

" As you wish ! " she finished by agreeing, and went deliberately to the door. He opened it, with bent back. She had already passed the threshold and had her foot on the landing, when seizing her by the wrist he pulled her backwards so brusquely that she almost fell down. In a weeping tone he implored her :

" No ! not like that ! Let us leave each other good friends. Another instant ! Pardon ! I have not done you any wrong, have I ? "

She remained mute, standing in front of him, with her cruel smile curling her lip up. Putting his arms round her, he drew her to the couch, made her sit down, and sat at her side. His face got congested, his eyes dilated, and his nostrils quivered, in the madness of his passion. She took his head, and crushed it against her bosom. He closed his eyes, breathing in the fatal perfume. With trembling eyes, he lightly touched her cheeks. She pushed him away a little, and tenderly smiled at him. Bending his head backwards, she gave him a long kiss, a moist kiss, which filled him with an unspeakable languor. She unbuttoned him, and began to frig him. Her light fingers gently put him into a sweet dream. He swooned : the sighs, and cluckings were stifled under this endless kiss. Her powerful and gentle hand excited him to delirium. All his body, stiffened, longed for delight. He groaned :

" Anna ! Anna ! Make me spend ! "

She kissed him again, sucking his lip, whilst her perfidious hand exasperated his nerves.

Suddenly she drew back, and left him.

He remained alone upon the couch.

As through a mist he saw her, upright in front of him. She smiled and examined him curiously. His balls tightening, quivered, the mucous membrane contracted spasmodically, and George collapsed. His hand wandered — and the sperm sprang out between his clenched fingers.

Despair and irritation, mingled with disgust, immediately swept over him. He readjusted himself in silence. Anna laughed, a strident and mocking laugh.

"That is the first lesson. You will come and see me again in a fortnight. And I am not afraid you will be faithless to me. Your hand will bring me to your mind!"

He heard her, his lips tightened, and quite incredulous, he felt relieved after she had gone. But little by little there grew in him a strange uneasiness, a vague desire, more and more haunting. He well knew this lust, this smarting of the mucous membrane, all the vain ardour in the inertia of the erectile nerve. It was thus that he suffered when she frigged him. But now it was quite another thing, sicklier and more depressing, with a more frantic desire for the supreme satisfaction. An hallucination haunted his brain, which was peopled with erotic images. He saw Anna in front of him, in her corset and little petticoat, studying her grimaces before the glass. Then he saw her naked, in the most lubric attitudes, with her backside frisking about. He heard her voice, that voice so sweet and penetrating, with its deep timbre, that imperious voice with its slow inflections: "Spend! I wish it!"

Scared, he ran to the Avenue du Bois.

"Madame has just gone away," the soubrette Claudine declared. "What, did not Monsieur know?"

"But where has she gone to then?"

"Madame has not left her address. She merely said that she should not return for a fortnight."

The soubrette did not lie.

The Russian had returned. Like a whirlwind he had traversed the whole of Europe. In the most desolate capitals he had tried the most dissimilar pleasures. And Anna's image, interposing, had tarnished all his orgies. The remembrance of her magic hand gripped him without respite. He felt subjugated, vanquished, without any possibility of resistance. From Constantinople, where the Asiatic refinements seemed to him insipid, he had made one day's bound to Paris. He at once sent Anna ten thousand francs and a despairing letter, grotesque through its excess of respect.

She replied to him by a single word: "Come!"

He hastened there. Kneeling, he deliriously suppli-

cated her to abandon herself to him. Without replying, she worked at his body, exciting him to madness,
mingling bites with her kisses, and caresses with
scratches. Then naked, on his knees, with joined
hands he again implored her, whilst bending over him
she pinched his nipples, and twisted his balls. Suddenly, leaving him, she ordered :

" Kiss my feet and frig yourself ! "

Confused, he obeyed. He rolled his eyes furiously,
seized himself brutally, and licked his tamer's shoes.
Then he began to howl, " I cannot ! I cannot ! "

She insisted, making the crystal of her voice vibrate :
" You must ! I insist on it ! "

He spent, bellowing, " Yes ! Everything—everything
that you wish. Everything for you, mistress. Darling
mistress ! "

He **had** dressed again, discomfited, meditating on his
disappointment, when Anna attacked him again. He
was speedily revived. She pushed him on a chair,
seating herself on his knees with a leg on each side,
and turning her back to him. Her vigorous croup put
him in erection. He felt a new happiness, and spent
deliciously. He kissed her hands fervently, and begged
her to fly from Paris with him. A fortnight only : and
he offered her a cheque for one hundred thousand francs.
She accepted. Immediately after seeing George she
rejoined the Russian, and went with him to bury them-

selves at Barbizon, in the middle of the forest.

Filled with an immense despair, George went home. He felt the inevitable: Anna had spoken the truth. The pupil remembered his first lesson. Already he had learnt, and knew.

George tossed himself off on his knees, before his mistress's portrait.

That evening he went to the pleasure houses, the brothels, in search of a woman. At last he saw a girl with an attractive face, and plump and slender. Anna's type. He went upstairs with her. Complaisantly, the girl worked her hardest, but he could not get a cockstand.

When he was alone in bed, he again frigged himself. But as he discharged, fervently repeating his mistress's name, he heard a movement in the next room. The nun, who was watching over his wife's corpse.

Next day was the funeral.

He imagined that Anna would come, and the thought of this insolence kindled his anger. But when he saw her nowhere in the church, he was rather disappointed. The odour of the incense upset him. He thought that if the priests could have taken his mistress's perfume to intoxicate the faithful, there would have been a recrudescence of faith. Whilst behind the bier he mechanically let go the hands of his young daughters. Stealthily he drew a coin from his pocket, wishing to know if she

would consent to give herself to him, if at least he would
have a kiss. The two weeks went by.

But he had to wait. With death in his soul he waited,
until Claudine arrived. She showed him into the boudoir,
where he found Anna who, with slippers on her feet and
quite naked, was lying with her backside in the air on
a bearskin rug. She turned, and re-turned herself, in
the most lascivious poses, kneading George under the
influence of her sombre glance. He stammered, crying
out his sufferings. How many times he had tossed
himself off, his repulsion for every other woman. And
he offered her his fortune for a night of love. In her
quiet voice she refused :

" No, besides have I not taught thee to suffice thyself? Frig thyself ! "

Misery wrung his heart. Tears ran down his cheeks,
without his dreaming of wiping them away.

" At least, may I see you ? "

" Certainly ! Everyday you will come and take my
orders."

He went away, burning with fever, in haste to be
alone, to frig himself even to prostration, and stupefied
torpor of mind and body.

Next day he stood mute with astonishment when he
saw her appear, her head wreathed with orange flowers,
dressed all in white, covered with lace, and with a long
bridal veil.

" What do you think of me ? "

He did not reply, surprised at the mascarade, and disconcerted above all by her demeanour full of candour, aud her air at the same time virginal and vulgar.

" A rehearsal ! I wanted thee to judge of the effect ! It is thus you will see me in six weeks, when you lead me to the altar."

He burst out, full of wrath, his voice vibrating with conviction.

" What are you thinking of ? Knowing you as I do ? You are absolutely mad ! Listen—I have only loved one woman—she is dead. As for you, I have only the feeling of the flesh. That won't last ! What would there be left then ? I should kill you ! "

She laughed, with her bad laugh, shrill and mocking.

" Imbecile ! Triple idiot ! You no longer see clearly ! The more I have given you, the more you wish to have. You have got me in your blood, in your nerves, in your skin—you will die of it ! "

" I would rather be castrated ! "

" So be it ! Spend then with what's left to you. Undress yourself."

He tried to get away from the influence of her look, and wished to flee, but in spite of himself, with involuntary movements, the stiff movements of an automaton, he took off his clothes.

She did not even need to speak, to make him approach : her eyes drew him, and continued to direct him. She remained dressed. Her slender body sheathed in its white bridal costume. Her forearms alone showed her flesh. She made him grovel to the fauteuil.

"I will make a good husband of you immediately, and put you in your place—beneath my feet."

She frigged him with her thin shoe. Confronted with the virginal apparel, he felt a new sensation. A bitter enjoyment, through which, during the pleasure, the shock of his misery persisted.

He caressed with a timid hand the vigorous and fine leg, moulded in its white silk stocking. He was fascinated with the to-ing and fro-ing of the dainty shoe, and discharged keenly.

"Lie down! All thy length!"

He obeyed. She crouched over him. Whilst she offered to his mouth the tastiest of tit-bits, she pinched his nipples, his loins, and his balls, and made him become erect again. She frigged him roughly, crushing the gland in her palm. She had thrown the long train of her dress over her arm. George's glance, lost in all these snows, concentrated itself on a pearly, living whiteness : the nudity of her marvellous bottom, showing through the opening of her drawers.

She pissed. Under the control of her hand, he lapped greedily. She farted. He sniffed it in. She shit. He spent in a convulsion. She cleansed him.

146

The Mistress and the Slave

"What am I?"—"You are my mistress! My good and sweet mistress! My well-beloved mistress!" —"And thou?"—"I am thy slave—thy humble and submissive slave!"—"Why dost thou refuse to obey?" —"I will obey! Mistress, adored mistress, I beg of you, for pity's sake, give me the alms of love! Your body, your sweet noble body! My sainted Anna, give me assuagement! If you knew how I suffer!"—"I know! And we will make love when thou art my husband. I will give thee delicious nights."

He went away, all irresolution banished. He decided that to wish to resist would be a folly. Suicide alone could save him. He thought of it. But already this burning, sickly, lancinating desire which the sorceress hand excited, obsessed him. He was afraid of dying before obtaining one of these delicious nights which she had promised him.

But next day, in a lull, a moment of lucidity, he transferred to an Assurance Company eight hundred thousand francs, his daughters' dowry. Henceforth, whatever might happen to him, he was easy in mind, sure that this money would belong to his children.

He hastened the preparations. The banns were published. The contract was signed. The bride had the management and disposal of the fortune. The papers spoke about the wedding presents, and enumerated their pomp. The wedding was at Saint-Philippe-du-

Roule.   In the naive and aisles a strange company
assembled.   A public which one rarely sees in Paris
churches, on the days of fashionable weddings.   Her
Belleville comrades.   They had come down with their
trollops to see it!   And the fashionable world were
unanimous in praising the bride's manner, her perfect
behaviour, her tact, and the degree of her emotion.
Neither too much nor too little.   No one thought of
jeering.   They even found it quite natural that she wore
orange blossoms.

When they were in the nuptial chamber, George, who
had matured a plan, slyly approached Anna.   Suddenly
he sprang forward, and holding her arms against her
body, he planted a rough kiss on her lips.   She raised
her leg, and with little muffled blows, she frigged him
with her knee.   Limp and conquered, he let go.

" Idiot ! do you think then there is anything changed ? "
He remained speechless.

" Undress thyself ! "
In an instant he was naked.

" On thy knees !   Don't move ! "
She went out.   He stayed kneeling in the same place,
scarcely daring to bend on his heels to relieve his
stiffened thighs ; straightening himself quickly at the
slightest sound.   Nearly an hour went by.   She returned
with Aïscha, the negress.   Both were naked.   George
again uttered a groan, and thought he was going to

faint when he saw an enormous dildo pointing from Anna's belly.

"Hein! What do you say to that? A maidenhead must be taken on a wedding night, so I shall take yours. Come on! Houp! On the bed, on all fours!"

He got on it, and placed himself as she wished. And he cried with anguish under the shocks of the instrument. Pain took away his cockstand. But Aïscha, passing her head between his legs, sucked him forcibly. He had to spend.

"Dirty beast! How he bleeds! See how he's filthied the sheets! Lie down, there, under the coverings!"

She sent Aïscha away, put on a silk chemise without sleeves, and lay down with him. At the same time she changed her tone, and became playful and tender. She dressed his wounds, anointed them with vaseline, and caressed him sweetly, filling his mouth with her pointed tongue. He sucked it devoutly. She gave him a delirious night. Her tongue frisked everywhere, revived him, and prepared him for the lists of love.

But next day she asked for the keys of the safe; and she had a fit of silent cold rage when she found that he had placed his daughters' dowry in safely.

Suddenly she burst out!

"Shit! This will teach me to put confidence in men!"

She raised two fingers, spat on the ground, and trod on it.

"My young man, you have just six months to live. It is I who tell you this. I shall frig thee to death! If I lie, I am no woman! You have suffered? It is nothing to what I shall make you do. But first you shall return me what you have stolen from me."

She had the horses put in. George had to follow her to the offices of the Company where he had secured his daughters' dowry. When she found that nothing could be done, Anna did not own herself beaten. George had to sign a life assurance proposal for a million francs!

That very evening he was exiled from the conjugal couch, and relegated to another room.

Henceforth he was assailed by strange pleasures, tortured, martyrised without a truce. Anna did not spare him a single blackguardly trick. She frigged him till the blood came, for a nothing, and inflicted on him the supreme humiliation, soiling his face with her excretions. She was often assisted by Aïscha, a robust and skilful accomplice. He experienced all the tortures which excite. Flagellation with a whip, with a cat-o-nine-tails. with rods, with nettles, with a switch bristling with pins. Enormous cupping-glasses were applied to his belly, sucking and swelling his prick and balls. Blisters were placed on his nipples and along his spine.

Anna tied him up and went out. For hours Aïscha and the maid, Claudine, rubbed, pinched and beat him. Then they tickled his loins and balls with peacocks' feathers. When Anna came back, she made him spend by a few jerks of her wrist.

But he grew exhausted. Spermatorrhoea had come, preventing any vigorous erections. His prick remained flabby, and he scarcely had an erection at the moment when he spént. Then he emitted a few drops of a clear viscid sperm, which dribbled out.

Meanwhile Anna didn't trouble herself, but received anyone who pleased her. And those, above all, pleased her who paid heavily. Immediately she got the money she ran to show it to George. With a gay air, she told how she had earned it, without omitting a detail. With a devilish animation, she imitated the paying lover, his attitude, his supplicating voice, his passionate exclamations. He received equally at her table and in her bed, lovers who did not pay. All of them a cheap lot: fine counter-jumpers. She made George treat them with the greatest politeness, although she permitted herself, in her husband's presence, every indecent familiarity. Sometimes, at night, she left the bed of adultery for a moment, and went to find George. He would be sleeping with a heavy feverish sleep, sweat glueing his hair to his temples. She drew off the coverings, and frigged him. Waking with a start, he cried for mercy.

" Darling mistress, I am so tired ! "

She did not heed him, but squeezed tighter, pressing on the bridle, and hastening the movement. Whilst her hand was draining the sources of life, she boasted of the delights of love.

" It is so good ! oh, it is so good ! Two people who like each other together. Do you see ? There's nothing real but that."

"Anna, hold your tongue."

" You 're not afraid ! So I've to hold my tongue ! You 're no longer my slave then ? "

" Oh, yes. Mistress, dearest mistress ! "

" Spend ! I want to see your spunk and your blood ! "

" Anna ! Mistress ! If you would only——"

" What ? "

" These delights ! This love ! Come into my bed ! "

" Idiot ! Don't you know what you are like ? Even if I consented, what could you do ? Why, look ! It is all limp, and gone to ruin."

He wept. The silent and obstinate snivelling of children who are in great trouble.

He no longer went out. With empty head, and extinct memory, he turned into a nonentity. Anna attended to his business, and made him sign all indispensable documents.

The six months which she had fixed were drawing to a close. One night when she came in she found

Aïscha and Claudine, who, following her orders, were rubbing and kneading George, heating his body for hours past. They had even applied moxas[1] on his loins, pieces of burning cotton-wool, the combustion of which they hastened by blowing on them.

They turned him round, and re-turned him, attacking above all the loins which they massaged together. Then, whilst Claudine slipped behind him, supporting him in a sitting position and fingering his scalp, the negress excited the glands at the fold of his groins by pinching them.

They again changed his position, making him lie on his stomach. Claudine's hand, leaving his scalp, lightly but insistently fingered his spine, striving to reanimate his nerves.

He lay inert, scarcely quivering from the keen attacks, when Aïscha bit his balls. His eyes were gloomy, his look fixed, his body was emaciated, and his figure was so pale that it looked like wax.

Anna approached him:

" Eh, well! so you're rebelling again, you don't want to spend?"

He bent his head down, confused, with the foolish look of a child caught in doing mischief.

---

[1] A moxa is a woolly soft substance burnt on the skin to produce an ulcer: a cautery.

"You *shall* spend! Besides, to-day is *the* day! You know well enough—you have got to die!"

"Darling mistress!"

"What good will it do thee to live? You can no longer fuck me! Shall I make you spend—as you have never yet spent?"

She undressed herself.

"Look at my beautiful arse. How good the smell of my neck is. Here! get drunk, dirty bugger! Sniff at my pussy. My arms, which you love so much, are round and firm. My leg is pretty, isn't it? Don't you remember the first time in the faubourg when I tossed you off? You didn't wish to spend, but I showed you my leg. And you came without my touching you. Eh, pig! How you spent! And do my eyes no longer please you?"

She enveloped him with her sombre look, her lustful glance, the promise of carnal paradise, the enjoyments of ecstacy.

He looked at her. She had come from the arms of a lover. Fatigue had sharpened her perfume, and her freckles made holes in her dull whiteness. Luxury oozed from her. Her velvety eyes—brown gems—had never shone with a more lascivious, more troubling, sweetness. A shiver ran through him. A light flashed in his eyes. The blood slightly mounted to his pale cheeks.

154

" Beloved mistress ! Sainted Anna, let your will be done ! "

She made a sign to Aïscha, who buckled the dildo round her, and sat on a chair. She thrust George on to the knees of the negress. Claudine tied his hands behind his back, and set herself to suck his nipples, and pinch his groin. He shuddered when the dildo penetrated, and cried out :

" Oh ! la ! la ! It scorches me ! "

Anna interrupted :

" Will you stop quiet ? Will you ? Here's a fuss about nothing ! Because I put a little Spanish fly on the end, and this good Aïscha has pushed it into your backside—how sensitive you've got ! "

" Mistress—my good mistress—your hand ! "

Anna took his prick and balls in her left hand. The prick was limp and stunted, the balls tiny, with flabby scrotum. The first finger of her right hand penetrated into the urethra, enlarging it, forcing it, tapping, and sinking into the canal, with a slow and continued forcing movement. George's features became drawn, his breath whistled, with a desperate complaining ; the groaning, more and more feeble, of a beast wounded to death.

The nail tore the mucous membrane, and ravaged his testicles.

She ordered :

"Spend!   I wish it!"

George jerked upwards.   His head rolled on Aïscha's shoulder, and his look curdled into a glassy stare.

Anna pulled her finger out.

A jet of blood sprang out, hiding some drops of fluid which were sperm.

THE END

DELECTUS BOOKS

"The world's foremost experts on titillating tomes" - Arena.

A GUIDE TO THE CORRECTION OF YOUNG GENTLEMEN
BY A LADY.

The ultimate guide to Victorian domestic discipline, lost since all previously known copies were destroyed by court order nearly seventy years ago. A cult hit in the U.K., fast becoming so in the U.S. "Her careful arrangement of subordinate clauses is truly masterful." *The Daily Telegraph.* "I rate this book as near biblical in stature" *The Naughty Victorian.* "The lady guides us through the corporal stages with uncommon relish and an experienced eye to detail...An absolute gem of a book." *Zeitgeist.* "An exhaustive guide to female domination." *Divinity.* "Essential reading for the modern enthusiast with taste." *Skin Two.* Delectus 1994 hbk 140p with over 30 illustrations. £19.95

THE ROMANCE OF CHASTISEMENT
OR, REVELATIONS OF SCHOOL AND BEDROOM, BY AN EXPERT

A renowned rare and elegant collection of verse, prose and anecdotes on the subject of the Victorian gentleman's favourite vice: Flagellation! We have published a complete facsimile of the rare 1888 edition, the first for over a hundred years. "One of the all time flagellation classics." *The Literary Review,* "In an entirely different class...A chronicle of punishment, pain and pleasure." *Time Out.* "A classic of Victorian vice." *Forum,* "A very intense volume...a potent, single-minded ode to flagellation." *Divinity,* "A delightful book of awesome contemporary significance...the book is beautifully written." *Daily Telegraph.* "Stylishly reproduced and lovingly illuminated with elegant graphics and pictures.....written in a style which is charming, archaic and packed with fine detail." *The Redeemer.* Delectus 1993 hbk 160p. £19.95

THE PETTICOAT DOMINANT
OR, WOMAN'S REVENGE.

An insolent aristocratic youth, Charles makes an unwelcome, though not initially discouraged pass at his voluptuous tutoress Laura. In disgust at this transgression Laura sends Charles to stay with her cousin Diane d'Erebe, in a large country house inhabited by a coterie of governesses. They put him through a strict regime of corrective training, involving urolagnia and enforced cross-dressing in corsets and petticoats to rectify his unruly character. First published in 1898 by Leonard Smithers' "Erotica Biblion Society", Delectus have reset the original into a new edition. "Frantic...breathless...spicy...restating the publisher's place at the top of the erotic heap." *Divinity.* Delectus 1994 hbk 120p. £19.95

120 DAYS OF SODOM
ADAPTED FOR THE STAGE BY NICK HEDGES FROM THE NOVEL BY THE MARQUIS DE SADE.

T he award winning play now available from Delectus, featuring stills from the London production and a revealing interview with the director. "A bizarre pantomime of depravity that makes the Kama Sutra read like a guide to personal hygiene." *What's On.*, "A brilliant stylistic creation." *City Limits*. "If you missed the play, you definitely need to get the book." *Rouge*. "Unforgettable...their most talked about publication so far." *Risque*. Delectus 1991 pbk 112p. £6.95

PAINFUL PLEASURES

A merican classic originally published in 1931 this book is an anthology of writing on discipline and corporal punishment administered by stern ladies to unruly young men and women. Delectus have produced a complete facsimile edition with the original 18 art deco line drawings by Francis Heuber.

The contents include a discussion on punishment, eight genuine letters and several short stories including "The Adventure of Miss Flossie Evans", "The Extraordinary Courtship of Hector Demerre" and "Discipline at Parame". The latter's plot in particular underscores the books themes: "How the magnetic personality of Cousin Gretha bought Elsie and Peter to meek and prompt obedience before this dominating young woman, thanks to the severity of the punishments she imposed; and how this stern and uncompromising disciplinarian succeeded in promoting their widely different careers." Delectus 1995 hbk in an imperial purple d/j 288p. £19.95

MODERN SLAVES
CLAIRE WILLOWS

T his superb full length novel relates the story of young Laura who is sent from New York to stay with her uncle in England. However, through a supposed case of mistaken identity, she finds herself handed over to a mysterious woman, who had engineered the situation to suit her own ends. She is whisked away to an all female house of correction in darkest Thurso in the far north of Scotland where she undergoes a strict daily regime under the stern tutelage to various strict disciplinarians. A beautiful facsimile reproduction of a classic from the golden Decade of American erotica including 10 superb art-deco style line drawings. Delectus Books 1995 hbk in an imperial purple d/j with black endpapers 272p. £19.95.

MEMOIRS OF A DOMINATRICE
JEAN CLAQUERET & LIANE LAURE

An elegant and aristocratic Governess recalls her life and the experiences with the young men in her charge. Translated from the French by Clair Auclair & Valentine Day from the French edition first published The Collection des Orties Blanches in Paris during the 1920s. Illustrated with reproductions of the 12 Jim Black drawings from the original French edition. Delectus Books 1995 hbk 140p. £19.95 (Due June/July 1995)

EROTICA, SEXOLOGY & CURIOSA - THE CATALOGUE

Delectus are the only global specialists selling quality rare, antiquarian, and second hand erotica by mail order. Our unique catalogues are dispatched quarterly to over 5000 customers in over 50 countries worldwide. Prices range from £5.00 to several thousand pounds representing the finest erotic literature from the last three hundred years in English, French, German and Italian including large selections from Olympia, Luxor & Grove Press. "Mouthwatering lists for serious collectors...decidedly decadent." *Risque*, "The leading source for hard to find erotica" *Screw*. "I have never seen a catalogue so complete and so detailed. A must" *Secret Magazine*. "One of the largest ranges of old and new erotic literature I have ever seen." *Fatal Visions*.

For our current catalogue send: £2.50/$5.00 Payment accepted by cheque, cash, postal order, Visa, Mastercard, JCB and Switch. Send to:

Delectus Books, Dept. M,
27 Old Gloucester Street,
London, WC1N 3XX, England.
Tel: 0181.963.0979
Fax: 0181.963.0502.
Mail order business only.
Trade enquiries welcome.

COMING SOON:

There's a Whip in my Valise, The Whippingham Papers, The Strap Returns: New Notes on Flagellation, Frederique: The Story of a Young Man Raised as a Young Woman, Lustful Lucy, The Amorous Widow & many more.

FURTHER PUBLICATIONS due in the next few months - see our full catalogue for further details.